CROW JAZZ

CROW JAZZ

short stories

LINDA ROGERS

Mother Tongue Publishing Limited
Salt Spring Island, BC
Canada

MOTHER TONGUE PUBLISHING LIMITED
290 Fulford-Ganges Road, Salt Spring Island, B.C. V8K 2K6 Canada
www.mothertonguepublishing.com
Represented in North America by Heritage Group Distribution.

Book design by Mark Hand
Cover design and interior crows by Rick Van Krugel
Typefaces used are Bookman Old Style and Plaza.
Printed on Antique Natural, 100% recycled
Printed and bound in Canada.

Mother Tongue Publishing gratefully acknowledges the assistance of the Province of British Columbia through the B.C. Arts Council and we acknowledge the support of the Canada Council for the Arts, which last year invested $157 million in writing and publishing throughout Canada. Nous remercions de son soutien le Conseil des Arts du Canada, qui a investi 157$ millions de dollars l'an dernier dans les lettres et l'édition à travers le Canada.

LIBRARY AND ARCHIVES CANADA CATALOGUING IN PUBLICATION

Rogers, Linda, 1944-, author
Crow jazz / Linda Rogers.

Short stories.
Issued in print and electronic formats.
ISBN 978-1-896949-65-9 (softcover).--ISBN 978-1-896949-68-0 (PDF)

I. Title.

PS8585.O392C76 2018 C813'.54 C2018-901251-X
C2018-901252-8

RECYCLED
Paper made from recycled material
FSC® C103567
FSC www.fsc.org

Aunty, don't let the devil use your brain.

—ADVICE FROM NIGERIAN WRITER
MAZI NZUBECHUKWA OKOYE

for our nesting children
and loved ones navigating the journey home,
and for Gordon Smith, dear teacher and friend
who understood that painting with words was an option

A BLESSING

This is her blessing, world without end, one story after the other, every one in a different key. She's all ears, tucked in, curled up in her Capsula Mundi, ready for lift-off, the rapture, maybe to a sacred forest, her former selves, nurse logs, rotting, *panis angelicus*; the holy *terroir*, her sinister smalldogs, little feet turning out, stirring up what comes next. She's swallowed her fairy suitcase filled with baby teeth, waits for her cue, the obladi/oblada aubade, morningsong. It's always morning, always the twitter of birds waking up, the idea of stretching into new bodies, this time, she hopes, an evergreen, her roots eating through compost, secrets and lies shared by the trickster, while her leaves reach up to the light. This time, she prays in her pervious shell, let's forgo consonants. This time, let's embrace the legato of vowels, the locus of beautiful dances, Sufis and ballerinas, green shoes growing like vines, Pinocchio's nose. Who will be the new fact-checker, the puppet or the ventriloquist? Who will be the new whisperer, Crow again, really, or maybe cosmic lips, goddesses moving her branches? She loves green sticks that sing, children in playgrounds, a murmuration of swallows, crows throwing their voices. Lalalalalala, life goes on. Inside the newtree, She.

CONTENTS

THE RANGER

He loves his fly swatter. It isn't exactly a swatter, more of an exterminator. It has criss-cross wires and batteries with a switch. When he hits things, they pop and fry. You can smell them, not quite bacon, more like burning hair. Once I leaned in too close to blow out my candles and turned into one. THAT was a birthday.

I was a curious morsel, thin enough to slip between trees and take note of transgressions in the woods, things like live burial and extra-marital sex, and I knew that a lot of famous people had died on their birthdays. The birthday list is hugely and I knew it by heart, up to the day I forgot everything and started again. I can still rattle off a few: Shakespeare, Sidney Bechet, Milton, FDR, Raphael, King Kamehameha V and Machine Gun Kelly.

Funny details are how I remembered facts. For instance, Liszt had moles on his face, and Beethoven had a horn for hearing music. The day I forgot everything and started again was, as it happens, my birthday, which started like all others. My parents, having totalled their first car on a bumpy road designated to abort my journey, were people who hated to be reminded of failure.

Since I was one of the few, my most irritating qualities being my tenacity and genetic predisposition to truth telling, my anniversaries were usually discrete.

On this occasion, I was given one dollar and a brown paper bag with one apple, one unpeeled carrot, one sandwich, two slices of pale white Wonder Bread with bologna and mystery mayo with colourful chunks that looked like vomit, one cellophane package of Dad's Cookies and a doughnut man with no sexual appendage for my anniversary picnic. So why was my doughnut a man? I asked, of course. Why wouldn't I? Why couldn't it be a doughnut woman? Or girl.

I licked the glaze between his her legs first, and there were no clues, no taste of male or female, no sudden erection, and no flash flood. Then I bit, revealing my interesting dentition, two front teeth that could, as my father said with a smirk, "eat an apple through a picket fence."

I inherited those teeth. They came with a fastball. He'd lost his in a baseball accident, and I got them back in an orgasmic collision. When he reached up to catch a fly during a major league tryout, he looked at the sun and the ball hit him square in the mouth. So Dad became a lawyer. I always thought "mouthpiece," gangster slang for lawyer, meant a washed-up baseball player with false teeth who'd missed his true vocation and went to work for crooks.

My father was also a golfer. He was the guy who brought in the clients because the rich klutzes who hired him thought a fellow who could hit a ball was on the ball. That might have been true. He golfed with lots of famous people, the president of the United States (the one who played football without a helmet), Zsa Zsa Gabor's husband, Bing Crosby. Bing Crosby recommended him to Errol Flynn, my mother's childhood hero, who phoned up the night he was busted with a fourteen-year-old. My parents were out. I took the call. Errol was in the jug, and he needed my dad, who turned up hours later in his party clothes, on that occasion, tails. He'd been dancing with the Queen. Two days later, Errol died of a heart attack.

My mother told me sudden death was what happened to old men who slept with little girls. That was all she ever told me about sex. I could, if not careful, end up with an old dead man on top of me, and that would absolutely ruin my debutante year.

I was still smart as a whip then, smart enough to memorise the licence plate numbers of all the perverts who cruised Chancellor Boulevard offering rides to little girls, smart enough to know when adults were telling the truth and when they lied, which was most of the time.

Who wouldn't want a kid like that out of the house, playing in the woods, making forts and taking notes on woodland behaviour? I don't blame them. They say the truth shall set you free, but my dad knew better. All his clients in jail knew better. Certainly Errol Flynn did in the jail beyond reckoning. There is no word for swashbuckling in the Hell-cells where they lock up the pederasts.

I had a knack for pedophiles. It was as if my magnetic brain, filled with leached amalgam from multiple fillings, sent out signals. Fillings were free. My dad exchanged them for pro bono advice, and our dentist was a perv. And they came like moths to light bulbs. The problem was I never forgot a face, a voice or a licence number. After I overcame my artificial modesty (I read *Lady Chatterley's Lover* under the covers when I was six) and admitted "penis" was a word I could handle in court after denying I knew its meaning to a curious cop, I was your ideal witness: clean, focused, articulate.

They came in droves: in cars ("Want to play with my little dolly?"), in trucks ("Officer, that was a meat sandwich in my hand.") and out of the woods with their pants down. I was a fast runner and a hell of a high jumper thanks to ballet classes, but under normal conditions, could easily have been overtaken by a long-legged adult male. A man with his pants down is not so fast. Women are another matter, but that is a story for another day.

Nowadays I am not so adversarial, not the lawyer's daughter. I would hand over a life-sized doll and a pass to an enclosed comfort home for adults with inappropriate sexual urges. I have learned that jail without hope and joy is the solution to absolutely nothing, a barbaric solution to childhood trauma, and that people are not always what they seem to be.

The forest was the opposite of jail in my childhood days. There were no narcissistic parents battling for supremacy in my woods, no ugly noises apart from the occasional crashing intrusion of perverts and The Ranger, who collected lost balls and lost kids, mostly the light footsteps of woodland creatures and birdsong.

I built forts out of tree branches and ferns, which also served as spears for repelling whatever threat interrupted my sylvan meditations. Recently, an artist friend has been rediscovering forts, evidence of a lost civilisation of children who created alternatives to irrational authority and technological babysitters. She posted one on Facebook, and I swear the tipi-shaped twig structure was my framing, a survivor of rampant real estate development.

One of the premium places to build was in the woods surrounding the golf course. These woods had been cleared and offered fern-sprinkled glades already levelled for child homesteaders. The golf course was far enough from our mothers and close enough that we could make it home for dinner without getting lost.

My fort was stocked with provisions stolen from home, loaves of Wonder Bread, which I liked with the crusts torn off, comic books and the requisite jar of Vaseline for Night Revels. Night Revels involved undressing with friends on the Solstice, covering the body with petroleum jelly and dancing in the moonlight. This would be followed by games of "doctor," the proto-lesbian activity essential to every girl's development.

Except for urgent calls of nature, golfers avoided these zones, where sliced and otherwise random balls often landed. These balls were a danger to us, but danger, then as now, was thrilling. We were simultaneously in a war zone, surrounded by poisoned grass and foot soldiers of commerce preoccupied with doing business and whacking *gutta percha* to kingdom come and sometimes into sand traps.

Perverts, wild animals and wild balls aside, the real danger was The Ranger, who hunted lost balls in the margins of mid-century civilisation. I have no idea who gave The Ranger his honorific. Now, I suspect, it was not the course managers, with nothing to gain from a terrifying unkempt man lurking in the shade on Ladies Day, when women golfed. The Ranger may have come from my lexicon, which included references to The Lone Ranger, pale man on a pale horse who kept the law on the rough parameters of Indian Country and settlement with his cynical sidekick Tonto.

In those days, I thought the masked outlaw-man was OK. Later he achieved star status when I had the opportunity to watch his half-hour show in the lobby of a Stratford hotel with the also legendary Glenn Gould, who bought me ice-cream and drove me home in his red convertible after I hid myself in Row G during his sound check.

The Golf Ranger was no hero. The psycho-pale of some redheads, bald with a few ginger threads with wretched clothing, he carried a five iron, whacking low-lying plants and shrubs and scaring squirrels as he charged through the bush with his pack of feral hounds. He never spoke, just raised his club and shook it as I or we ran screaming to the safety of the highroad that ran parallel to the golf course, chased by yapping dogs, but only as far as the end of the trees. I was fast. My friends were fast, but we all knew about the disappeared.

On those long evenings of the full moon when we left by window (all my friends tried for a ground-floor bedroom or at least a room with a window that could be reached with a stepladder or high chair) and congregated in the forest, we told Ranger stories, repeated and embellished what we had heard from other kids. Rumour had it he boiled the golf balls and the kids in the same pot to make dog food. When he could stick a fork in the golf balls, then the kids were cooked. His dogs would never eat an underdone kid. That's how he got rid of the evidence.

When we saw dogs with bones, we trembled in fear. When we found bones buried in our gardens, we knew they were parts of a missing neighbour, some boy or girl who hadn't been fast enough, whose name was never spoken again. It was embarrassing for parents to lose track of kids, and so they kept the disappearances quiet.

"Fatso!" some kids yelled at other kids, not to be mean but to give a warning, "The Ranger's gonna getcha!" But not me. I read "sticks and stones" backwards. I knew words were powerful, and they could hurt.

"Fuck off!" I yelled at the dogs, and they understood, returning to their tyrant with tails between their legs, hugging the ground, I assumed, all the way home. "Home" I assumed was a rundown shack in the burbs with a whiskey still and a child fire burning night and day. The Ranger probably had a bushed scraggly wife and a handful of brats in rags, too thin to eat and black and blue like the McKenzie kids whose paediatrician father was later charged with abusing his patients and hitting children who were afraid of needles, and sent to jail forever and a day.

We set traps for The Ranger: holes covered with ferns, bear traps, decapitating wires and tempting dog-shit sandwiches wrapped in waxed paper, but he outsmarted us, coming and going as he pleased, always leaving with a bag full of hurt golf balls. If then were now, we'd have him on camera and social media, worldwide perv alerts.

Even though I was a junior detective who collected evidence for crimes reported in the *Vancouver Sun*, our conflict ended at the end of the woods. I was afraid to spy on The Ranger at home. That was too dangerous. He knew where I lived. I am remembering all this now, but there were decades when I couldn't. I just couldn't.

My birthday was on a Saturday, an all-clear day because The Ranger took weekends off, collecting all the lost balls Monday to Friday, after the frenzy of bogies and drunken swings that marked the release of businessmen from work at the office and the demands of children. God forbid they should take the kids swimming or out for a family hike. I really get it that the Hate Pumpkin needs to get away from his family and murder balls on his weekends away from high office.

My father gave me a silver dollar to chase The

Ice-Cream Man, possibly an unkind joke because I had never before managed to catch him. You had to hear the high notes, the ice-cream jingle, and then as now, I am not so good on the high register. My siblings warned me, and off I went, flying down the street with my shoelaces undone. *The Ice-Cream man, the Ice-Cream man*, I repeated the mantra. It was my birthday. I was going to buy an ice-cream sandwich.

After three blocks, the Ice-Cream Man stopped for a bunch of kids who were ready and waiting at the corner with their sweaty change. I sat down on the curb, catching my breath, cash in one hand, brown paper bag in the other, waiting my turn, and watched him serve Rainbow Popsicles and fruit slushies to the other kids, who joined me on the curb as they were served. Maybe it was the way he looked at me, the *I know who you are* look I saw in my worst nightmares. There was something familiar about the Ice-Cream Man, surface smiley and perky in his white uniform and hat at an angle with a top note of sinister in his little jingle. Something vile rose in my mouth and sat there. Something held me back.

Then he turned his back, and I knew.

The Ice-Cream Man was The Ranger. I dropped my money and my lunch and ran for the woods, took a shortcut, grabbing spears should he follow. I took a chance, like John Landy who lost the four-minute mile after turning around to see who was behind him, but The Ranger wasn't following. It was his day off. That made me one lucky puck, but not for long.

They say you can see death coming. It arrives in slow motion, like a ball aimed at your head, and that's where it caught me, right, as they say, in the middle of my forehead. My world spun and went black, an aperture slowly closing, then opening. I saw clouds in my sleep and the sun at the end. I heard angels singing.

I was knocked out cold. When I woke up, it was night, and because I am an intuitive creature, I found my way home to my cellmates and the babysitter. Our parents had gone out for the evening. My dinner was in the oven. I ate it and hurled, then, taking a hint from the sitter who was pointing at my head and laughing, I looked in the bathroom mirror. A golf-ball-sized goose egg.

"What happened?" she asked, but I had forgotten. In fact, I had forgotten pretty much everything, including the licence plate numbers of every pervert who drove by the university woods and the times tables. I even forgot it was my birthday.

Over the years, I have made do with scrapbooks and other memorabilia that pass for memory. I scan the alphabet to trigger lost names. Some things have surfaced unbidden, passing as stories filtered through crow gossip, the news media and my imagination. I start every account by saying, as memory serves me, in case it doesn't. Some people think I am a congenital liar.

These days, journalism and storytelling are under assault. I don't care, the truth set me free, and the truth is, I am a child of the forest freed from the past by the effect of one golf ball that landed smack in the middle of my forehead. I had the sense knocked out of or into me on my tenth birthday, and that explains everything. Eureka! Thank you Zeus for decades of ditziness, just what my father wanted in a daughter.

Just like the crack in my head ("There is a crack in everything/that's how the light gets in."), my tooth cracked without warning. There is a note on my dental chart that says, WATCH THAT MOLAR, but no one told me, or I wasn't listening, or I forgot on account of my brain injury. Little did I know that molar was the source of my leaks. Someone should tell the Deranged Rooster whose hens lay golden golf balls to have all his surrogates, escorts and aids checked by a dentist. Leaks can be involuntary, sometimes radioactive.

We were on the roof, having a beer. NO, I did not open the bottle with my teeth, although I have done stuff like that, just to prove I really was as stupid as my father wanted (Smart women never catch husbands, and there were already three, count 'em, three old maids in my family, all of them alleged lesbians.). All I did was sneeze, hard and loud, so hard I dislocated my jaw, and when my teeth clamped down, the tooth split in half. That is a small event in a life that includes witnessing the era of King Leer, but still, I noticed. My tongue groped around. Tongues magnify everything; but before I had a chance to locate the pebble in my mouth, I had swallowed it.

My fly-swatting husband suggested I wait with a colander to see if it emerged enamel, gold or amalgam.

We could save the situation if my rogue body part turned out to be a 10-karat nugget.

I said, "No way," and made an appointment with my dentist, who made a few jokes and a sensible decision. No prince, no crown. He fussed and drilled and made a huuugely filling, blocking the light with amalgam. "You never know. The world might end tomorrow." I worried that with the jarring, the rest of my teeth would fall out. If my body were programmed to reject foreign lumps of metal, I might choke on the filling and die in his chair. If the default mechanism failed, I might have to endure rape by the pain police, another extraction with the dentist's brogue braced in my crotch, drenched by a downpour of dental sweat, my gums broken and aching, rogue bits of root drifting to my brain where they would surely precipitate an aneurysm, the fatal stroke of fate.

"This might work," he said, and I hung onto the word "might" like a drowning person in a lake filled with piranhas. Might. I conjured the image of a mighty girl fighting back, hurling sword ferns at an army of men with drills. As it turned out, his solution was not only good enough, but even better. I started getting radio signals halfway through the procedure, and before I left the office, the crows were singing, most of my memory had been restored.

The first thing I remembered was The Ranger.

THE TEA PARTY

"Those who can make you believe absurdities can make you commit atrocities."
—VOLTAIRE

Moon, a girl of too many words way too many for an eleven-year-old, has been clammed up for a week. Her think position is head down, teeth tight, but this unnatural silence is unnerving.

The parent units are alarmed. "Wherefore art thou, Moon?" Windsong, our mother, tried teasing, but Moon has remained clenched, making a growling sound somewhere between purring and roaring, for a whole week.

"Meow?" I tried, my falsetto, a family joke because we sing the Rossini cat duet boy girl instead of boy boy, both of us comfy trebles.

"Moon, please. "I'm worried." Our mother is at the breaking point. She says my sister and I have fried her nerves with our hormonal behaviour. And now this.

"I think she's transforming." I am actually curious. Maybe we're hearing child labour, and Moon is getting ready to shed her skin and turn into something else, New Moon.

"Cat? Rabbit? Probably cat. Sounds like cat," I ask. This morning Moon is swinging and knitting, and I am standing behind her, pushing even though she is quite capable of managing two things at once without my help.

I check her bum for a tail emergent. No tail yet.

"Speak," I insist for the zillionth time. "Earth calling Moon. What's up?" I ask.

She surprises me by opening wide and freeing her first post-incident words, "I'm throwing a tea party for the Grim Brothers," she spits out, then puts on the brakes, kicking up dust, scuffing her shoes, a star demerit offence.

"When?"

"Today."

"Am I invited?"

"That depends."

Moon is my sister, but not always my confidante.

"You have certain deficiencies."

"Like?" I pause and revise.

Because we are the children of uber-grammarians, "like" is a word we are not allowed to use. "Like" is the crutch of the metaphorically challenged, and metaphor is everything to Moon.

"Such as?"

"Refusing to dress up on your boy days."

In the world of facts and alternative facts, that's a fact,

but aren't we flexible, temperate? We live in a temperate zone, where it rains every time a cloud hits a mountain.

I love rain. I worship rain. I love dancing in mud puddles and drinking rainwater straight up, straight from the sky. Look up! I love flushing the toilet, the deep gargle sound of the toilet throat, the tat of drips and drops hitting leaves, wet pavement and mud puddles, but the Grim Brothers' golden showers were so over the limit I wanted to break their heads on the sidewalk.

This behaviour scares me off girl days. I'm the one who watched in horror from the safety of the hedge when Moon's glasses fell off her face and bounced on the sidewalk.

Yes, we have pavement, concrete, impervious surfaces. The sidewalk defines our world. Inside is Paradise, the old Persian word, outside is traffic, cars in a hurry, bodies outlined in chalk, chalk for ingesting, nothing like rabbit skin glue. I know these things because Windsong made us read *The Rubaiyat* and is currently teaching us how to make paint.

Windsong struggles to keep us safe, now more than ever, now that bullying is empowered by the regime change, in our life circumscribed by whispering branches and squealing tires. Inside, I can ride my bicycle bareheaded. Outside, I have to wear a helmet. How's that for a metaphor, Moon?

"OK, Moon. You win. But don't forget we are persons, and persons are capable of intentional blindness."

I am a restless two-spirit kid, with two completely

separate minds, both of them able to decide when fight or flight is the better option. She's chosen fight, the blind leading as usual. It's like, there's that word again, wearing specs, one pair for reading the past, one pair for looking into the future.

"You are too smart for your own good, Sun." This is what the units say when we out-think them. We are home-schooled, unfettered, freethinking post-millennial brats if you believe the conventional wisdom, which isn't very smart these days, and we've been having conversational downturns, ever since the red-faced flop-tummied Red Queen turned out to be four giant babies screaming, "Off with their heads," and worse.

"Blindness," she says, "is involuntary."

"Not necessarily."

"Don't contradict me," she says in a perfect Windsong snit voice, gale force with salt in it," or I'll stick this needle in your boy bun."

"You expect a hot air leak?"

"Worse, way worse. You're so full of shit your eyes are brown." At least mine work, I think but don't say.

"You might miss and poke my eye out. Then where would we be?"

"Two blind nice."

"That's not very nice."

"It's a joke, stupid."

She's knitting with the spines of eagle feathers, and they have very sharp points.

"My feathers have magic." She points one at me. "I

could do a spell and turn *you* into anything I want."

"I am what I am," I say, "born two-spirit and staying that way. Do you *really* want to have a conversation about that?"

"You are an anomaly." She's proud of the word, proud of me. I can tell this whole tea party thing is her revenge sister act. Last Saturday the Grim Brothers bombarded us with slogans and peed on our fence, splashed the swing, even. When Moon ran to tell Windsong, her glasses fell off and she stepped on them. Today, I suspect, she has a plan.

"An anomaly you need to defend? Is it a tea party or a war party to defend my honour?"

"It isn't always all about you. I just want to teach them a lesson. In general. They've been pissing me off about a lot of things, the rabbits for one. The Grim situation is heating up."

"But revenge tastes better cold," I repeat one of Windsong's favourite proverbs. Windsong is a Buddhist. Another favourite is, "If you wait by the river long enough, the bodies of all your enemies will float by," but Moon clearly has no time for that.

"Don't let the devil use your brain," I have now shot off every arrow in my quiver, the last my favourite.

"Too late," she says.

She points her feet at the traffic and pumps her huge legs. Every time my sister tells a lie, her legs grow longer. Soon they will drag on the ground, and we will have to move her swing to a higher branch, or shorten the ropes.

"Watch out for the cars," I say. I don't blink again, because, if I lose focus, Moon will extend too far and lose her platypus feet and her pink patent party shoes, size eight already.

She has that fierce planning-the-campaign look. How many cups and saucers? Should the sandwiches be served crust on or crust off?

"Off with their crusts," she says out loud. The Brothers are greedy pigs, and Moon must be counting on her secret recipe, whatever that is.

"Rabbits aren't sluts. Rabbits aren't sluts," she chants, her voice getting higher and louder. Stitches fly off her needles as fast as rabbit sex, which we time with stopwatches and record in one of our infamous note-books. The Grim Brothers have threatened to catch our bunnies and put them in cages.

"Breed 'em and eat 'em. Off with their heads."

She swings, no hands, her feet sailing over the picket fence, touching the sky and missing the traffic by inches while her hands keep knitting. Back and forth, back and forth, my head moves with her. I hold my breath when she slows down and casts off, keeping her slippery angora act together. She's still got her feet, shoes, socks, ankles and toes on. She keeps knitting. The Cossacks are coming. They will deliver the Brothers to Moon's tea party in a basket of kitty litter, a Trojan pussy.

"We do have a problem." She stops the swing, dragging her shoes on the ground.

"What is it?" I am tired of standing here waiting for

the turn that never comes. Moon only gives up the swing when she has to pee, which she does in the bushes, quickly, using leaves for toilet paper, once stinging nettle, ha ha.

Our dad, Ocean, who plays the piano but not as well as Moon, says she swings like a metronome (Look out, I'm gathering likes, like it or not, an Ungrammarian). Back and forth is her game, always thinking, always knitting little things on her little needles, arms wrapped around the swing ropes.

"The Grim Brothers are carnivores. They eat meat."

"Egg is perfect, future meat, no excuses necessary."

"Pussies don't eat eggs."

"OK, tuna too."

"Naa." We both hate tuna fish sandwiches.

"How about shredded rooster?"

"Sometimes we have to compromise to get results."

"Who said that?"

"I think it was Windsong."

"She also says, 'You are what you eat,' Sun."

"We are not going to turn into chickens and fish, or carrots for that matter. The person she's quoting died of cancer. She was living on toxic organic bone meal."

"We could put bone meal in the sandwiches. I helped Ocean plant poppies and he put a handful in every hole, and there's some left over."

"We could give them bone meal enemas," my General muses. We both overheard Windsong tell Ocean she was thinking of having a tequila enema when Agent Orange declared war on Mexico. Our mother needs all the help she can get. My ambiguities have sent her to opioids, which constipate her. Life is complicated for Windsong.

"Logistically impossible. We can't hold them all down at once."

"Too true. Silly idea."

"So gay," I say. All my ideas are gay, she says, even though I am a two-spirit person. Not gay, gay and or girlie.

The Grim Brothers loathe my girl couture; give me the tiny finger whenever they pass our house. They're threatening to unfrock me, before capturing the rabbits, before they beat up all the kids with natural tans: the Geeks, the Afreaks, the Gooks, and the Hispanics.

This inspires my two-spirit central control mechanism and gives me a desperate brain wave. "We could feed them beans, *frijoles refritos*. That would blow their minds and..."

"No, no, no, *As ye feed, so shall ye eat*. We will have to eat whatever we feed our enemies, and I am sick of *refritos*."

"So tuna then?"

"No again, Sun. I will make the tea, and you will gather the rabbit food and the rabbits. Then you will help me serve the guests."

"Serve them right," I think. There is work to do.

"First we will set up the table together, the yugeliest tea party ever. That's when you will lure the rabbits to the shed and lock them in, while I make the sandwiches. When the Brothers arrive, I will put on the kettle, and you will help me serve. But you cannot sit down with us unless you put on a dress and a hat."

"Why?"

"Because it will piss them off."

"But I'm experiencing puberty, both kinds, different days. I don't want to wear a dress today."

"That's fine, but these people require homogeneity. Since they are all boys, we must be girls. They are not capable of reading your subtleties, your ambiguities. Besides, I am making hats for them. You will wear one too."

"What if one of them..."

"Grabs you by the pussy?"

"Yes."

"Trust me. That will make them crazy. Nothing beats grabbing a pussy and catching a snake."

"I get it, capture the Queen and we checkmate. Is that when the pussy riot begins?"

"There are one or two more moves in the game. Trust me."

By this, she means, she has options. If whichever brother grabs the pussy survives his homoerotic surprise, there will be another. Moon loves options: the handy brother and sister switch, her many Plans A and Plans B, which include compromise, but not capitulation. Never.

"We will save you *and* the diggers."

Moon and I are descended from Diggers, a protestant farming cult. In the Nineties, our parents, both religious nut cum hippy spawn, met in a commune that grew hemp and traded Columbian exports with Mexican drug dealers. Dig. Dig. Dig. They did well by the barter system, drugs for dust. Their work on the Mexican border, digging for drug lords, was so rewarding they were able to get out of the dig business, buy three beautiful acres and retire at the edge of the Rainforest.

They built our house, planted an orchard; and then the rabbits came and ate the bark. The bunnies were tenacious and greedy, so Windsong and Ocean locked them up in dream hutches with gardens and straw beds and collected their fur for spinning. Before long, they discovered the captured bunnies had Houdini DNA. They tunnelled their way out of jail and invaded the Grim Brothers' compound, enraging their parents.

The Grim parents built a fence, and our rabbits continued their rabbit business.

Wherever there is a wall, there is a way under or over it. In our diaries and maps of alternative facts, which we show to our psychologist, we have compiled circumstantial evidence that Mexican rabbits helped El Chapo burrow his way to freedom, temporary freedom because he has been recaptured and brought to New York for trial by a jury, he can only hope, of stoned Hispanics.

"You did your research." Our shrink was impressed.

"We're dead against walls," I told her.

The Grim Brothers have been building the biggest wall ever, a Great Wall, yuuge, between their house and ours. They've been piling up dirt and rocks and rusty car parts, burying broken glass and hurling insults.

"Gonna grab you by the pussy."

"PUSSY!" the three satirical crows on the fence sing in lock step.

"Moi? Good luck. I can't wait."

Moon is now off her swing, picking up swatches of pink from the ground where she dropped them and putting them in her knitting bag. "Four hats," she says. "Four boys."

"Hurry up. It's almost time."

"How do you know they will show?"

"I wrote an invitation they can't refuse, pricked my finger and sealed it in blood, then I nailed it to their front door. Look, I made two copies." She pulls a folded piece of paper out of her bag.

Moon DeBurgh Ronson
requests the presence of the Grim Brothers
at a chocolate fountain party
to discuss taxidermy
in the meadow
Saturday June 10, 2017, 3 pm
Party hats provided. Please leave knives, slingshots, peashooters, itching powder, fart cushions etc. with your mother, who will decide whether or not you'll get them back.

"Taxidermy?" I ask.

"Bait," she answers, grabbing the stair rail because her new glasses aren't ready yet, and she's making do with the old ones. "Now, you go bait the rabbits."

Summer's hardly started, but we already have baby carrots, radishes, lettuce and parsley in our rabbit-proof raised beds. I'm picking a big basket full, and the bunnies are noticing. I see them peeking through the chicken wire. I can almost hear them salivating.

The tool shed is a few steps away from the vegetable garden, and like Hansel and Gretel, (oops) I drop a few hors d'oeuvres on the path and I've got them. When I spread the feast on the concrete floor, they are all over it. All that remains to do is to wait until the shed is filled and then pull up the drawbridge. I take a moment to enjoy the improbability of turning the mopheaded Grim Brothers upside down and sweeping up when the rabbits are done eating and shitting in the shed before I lock them up.

I once wrote a song, "All we do the whole day through is eat and poo." "You're a poet," Moon said, the first time I sang it.

She's already setting the table in the meadow, a picnic bench made from a huge cedar that fell in a storm the year I was born. Ocean flattened the top with a chainsaw and used the part he cut off to make benches. The table seats twenty, and we have big family picnics on my birthday.

My sister was born in the winter, and she suffers from picnic party envy. This is her day.

She has covered part of the table with a linen tablecloth and is arranging six napkins, six place cards, six plates, and six cups and saucers, none of them matching. Moon is squinting, lining up the settings, which are more or less orderly. Her knitting bag sits by her place. Our corvid friends are lined up on a branch, waiting for a pitch fork to set them off.

"How come all their place cards say Grim?"

"Because they think with one mind and don't deserve names."

"No forks or spoons?"

"These people are barbarians," says Moon, spitting in a cup.

I follow her example and spit in three more.

"Get going," she says, "we're done here," and I head for the house.

En route I pick some more lettuce and take it in to Windsong, who is in the kitchen making mayonnaise.

"I think it is so nice that you kids are making overtures. Peace in our time. No one is all bad."

Wrong Windsong. Wrong. Wrong Wrong. NO PEACE WITHOUT JUSTICE. We are third-generation hippies, but, despite congenital blindness and pharmaceutical interference with our genes, we see more clearly than she ever did. Bad is bad. She is our history teacher, but she's blinder than Moon. I open my mouth to say something snarky, but Moon burns through the door and puts a sock in it.

"Time to get dressed, Sunny." She gives me a shove.

She's right. There is no point in questioning Windsong's artificially enhanced sunny ways. She does have the power to obstruct.

"I'm getting changed," I say.

"It's a girl day after all," Moon sings.

I find a dress laid out on my bed. Moon has decided for me. It is pink. It is girlie. It has a big puffy skirt with crinolines. I put on a slip and take out my boy bun. I brush my hair, attach a hairband with silk roses, paint on mascara and pink pearl lipstick and finally don the girlie dress and my gold sandals, a ladies nine from the thrift shop. I feel gorgeous, not confused. It is a girl day after all.

"Beautiful," Windsong says. I am. I walk in beauty like the night. In her heart of hearts, she likes girls best. I know it.

Windsong is cutting the crusts off the egg salad sandwiches and arranging them on a plate. Moon is slicing up fruit.

"Here," she hands me a bowl of strawberries, grapes and pineapple. "Ocean's setting up the fountain, and I will bring the chocolate and the tea."

Something sparks in my brain. It's the way she says chocolate, not in the dreamy creamy way. But all consonants, ch,c,lt. It could be code.

But my thoughts are drowned out by the sound of drumming. I look our the window and see brothers marching up the path around the house and down the trail to the meadow, banging pot lids with big wooden spoons, and chanting.

"Grab the pussies. Eat the rabbits. Off with their heads."

"I can stay," Ocean offers when we get there with our provisions.

"We're fine," Moon insists, but her voice wobbles. She places her Minnie Mouse teapot, her precious teapot from Disneyland, on the table next to her place, and waves our hovering helicopter parent off.

It's us and them. We have joined the deplorables.

"You have place cards," she says to her pot-banging guests, and then in a lower voice, "Do you need help with that?"

They put down their kitchen drums and sit. I take note of their dress code. Obviously, Windsong and the Grim Mother have exchanged words. The boys are wearing clean white shirts, and their ginger hair looks spat on, patted and parted. I have seen this many times. The Grim Brothers march to church every Sunday. This is their Sunday School uniform. They are Christian Soldiers, some kind of Baptists. The bad kind.

Moon adds the chocolate. The fountain is bubbling.

CH,c,lt tickles both my brains. I try not to smile as the Brothers, mesmerised by the fountain and the mountain of fruit, sit down obediently. We know they will eat and run.

Moon stands up. "There will be no more war. We will eat and play games."

"Eat!" The Grim boys yell in sync. They've really got the unison thing down, must be the Sunday School practice. I'm surprised they didn't learn to take turns there. It's impossible to get past the scrum around the chocolate fountain, so I don't bother. Nor, I notice, does Moon, who passes the almost full plate of egg sandwiches to me.

"Eat! Don't let these go to waste," she says with a wink and a wicked grin. "They seem to be going for the chocolate."

"Yes they are." The Grim Brothers grab handfuls of fruit, and the chocolate drips off their chins, staining their Sunday School shirts. There will be hell to pay with the Grim Mother.

"Plenty where that comes from," I agree. Let them fill their boots.

"Don't be so sure," Moon says. "I used it all up."

In moments, they've demolished the fountain. The fruit is all gone.

"Tea time," she says, "I'll be mother. She gets up and pours tea with a swizzle of honey at their places. This is some trick for a girl who can hardly see. I notice when she pours mine, it drips on the tablecloth. The tea makes a yellow stain.

"What kind of tea?" I ask and she answers, "Pure." Now I know what the Grim Brothers don't. "Pure" is what my mother calls her dying solution, a mixture of petals and uric acid.

The Grim Brothers are parched. They say the chocolate is salty but good. "It tastes like Hershey bars." One of them licks the fountain, and I wish it would freeze so his tongue would stick. Painfully.

"Finish the sandwiches," Moon says, "and let the games begin."

"What about the taxidermy part? " one of the feral boys inquires, "Liar, liar pants on fire, we came here to stuff your rabbits."

"Wrong," Moon tells him. "You came here to stuff yourselves, and we have kept our part of the bargain."

She instructs us to fold our napkins and cover our eyes. We're going to play hot and cold because she has hidden a giant surprise. "Yuuuge," she says. "The biggest ever. The treat of treats, and then the war will be over. No slagging, no grabbing, no beheading."

Four inbred morons, aged eight to twelve, versus two precocious sissies, twelve and thirteen. Of course they will win. They have already won. The war is already over. The Grims smirk at one another and put on their blindfolds.

Moon says, "Wait. I forgot the party hats." Moon puts an adorable pink hat on each Brother in turn. I'm off the hook because I'm wearing her hairband. Because I have not been ordered to fold my napkin and cover my eyes, I can see helicopters emerging from the weeds and circling the picnic table. They are carrying signs, four of them, one in each hand, all printed in felt pen.

Ocean is holding FEMPIRE STRIKES BACK! and SO BAD THE PARENTS ARE HERE, felt pens on cardboard. Windsong holds aloft CUNNING STUNTS and WATCH OUT! THESE PUSSIES SCRATCH!

Bravo parents! Brava! My chest swells with pride. I may not need breast augmentation after all. Thank you Windsong and Ocean. I lose concentration and in the confusion, allow the Grim Brother standing beside me to take a leap in the blindfolded dark. He fumbles between my legs and gets his answer.

Snake! I grab him back. The brother has a tiny erection. Of course.

"Grab her by the pussy." He squeezes out his feeble battle cry, and Windsong clobbers him with her CUNNING STUNTS sign while the others, intent on winning, follow my sister. Winning matters in the Grim Brother household, even when it means leaving casualties in the battlefield.

"Warmer," Moon shouts. They want the big reward so badly they keep following. My nearly blind sister, belting out "Warmer! Warmer!" leads them straight into the blackberries and stinging nettle, just like Brer Fox (like again).

"Hot!" Moon yells at the top of her lungs. They are tangled in scratch wounds, but my genius General has managed to keep herself free of the brambles.

The Grim Brothers shriek in pain. They tear off their blindfolds. They see each other, wounded boys in matching pink pussyhats shaped like vulvas. There is nothing huge waiting for them in the prickles, no candy store, no bright shiny toys, only scratches and blood, AND ADULT WITNESSES.

They look absolutely ridiculous.

"Who's the pussy now?" my sister says in a calm voice. "You pussies have been drinking my pee and you have eaten mass quantities of ex-lax (Yes! I get it. ex-lax is

Windsong's laxative of choice, her anti-opioid), and now you are going to pick up your mother's pots and pans and the wooden spoons she will use to spank you when she sees the condition of your Sunday School outfits, and you will get going before you start going because you are not going to use our bathroom."

The chanters are howling, making animal noises as they crash through the underbrush, taking the short-cut home. Having watched them scramble for food like a litter of deranged puppies, we can hardly imagine the scene in the Grim bathroom.

The two of us are laughing so hard we are in danger of losing it. We both get our panties down in time to pee in the comfort of our own bushes while Ocean volunteers to clean up the tea by himself in case the Grim Father comes after us with his fence post auger. What is the bother of tidying up compared the safety of his children?

We march back to the house, accompanied by Windsong, both kinds, and crow laughter. A storm may be whispering getting ready to roar, but we are armed and dangerous, and honour is on our side.

"Sorry about your ex-lax, Mum. It was used for a higher purpose."

"It sure was," she says.

"I hope Ocean remembers to let the rabbits out."

"Have we made the world safer for them?" My sister wonders.

"We'll see." Our mother might have found a renewed purpose in life.

THE CHILD CITY

They don't know I'm watching. That's what curtains are for, seeing and not being seen, or the opposite.

The curtain is falling on our marriage, no excuses, no reason. Maybe it's been there all along.

"I'm playing house," I've said on many occasions, excusing my febrile gusto for cooking and cleaning, my colour-coordinated clothesline, my weed-free garden, my compulsive needlework, and every play has a beginning, middle and end. Act 3.

It's a game of perfect symmetry, one Lego brick on another until someone stops breathing. First it was the babies that didn't want to live. Now it's me. Inhale like that, and the brick sticks in your throat. Believe me.

I started by throwing things in the fire, photographs with his face cut out, jewellery, my mother's black pearls.

I'm attracted to fire. Does that define our species, we who cook our meat? We are hunters, but isn't our definition of civility versus savagery "well done" as opposed to "rare"? I like my meat savage, with or without parasites; but then, how do you know; so many parasites are invisible.

It's dark outside, but the kids have flashlights with the trajectory of bullets in what we call the Garden of Eden, an acre of vegetables, orchards sloping to the estuary and fields dotted with sheep and evergreen high-rises, home to eagles and ravens.

Paradise.

And the children, undisturbed by torment, playing with Lego and Playmobil, building happy families and child cities. Just one ripple on the quiet pond of our existence, a childhood friend, no, more than a friend, a brother whose parents, alumnae of the Kuper Island Residential School, drowned in alcohol, choked on their own vomit, and left him in the care of the parish priest and a nun, and us, of course, because we were his rebound option, a safe haven with cookies and crayons and horses to ride.

He burned three churches before they caught him and put him in jail.

That was simple arithmetic, but the children needed to understand, "When you've been thrown in the fire, you start fires."

Once a rat came into our house and climbed a curtain. Don't they say, see one count twenty? They probably climb all the curtains while we sleep. Rats, cockroaches, the vermin tiptoe out of the dark and violate our dreams. There's no light on in the bedroom where I stand, looking down, watching my children scurry, life as we know it.

More like fireflies. I see Ku Klux Klan, riding with torches at night, burning crosses on lawns.

I had high fevers as a child, all of them turning into nightmares, terrifying fires: Nazis kindling their ovens with little children, Hansel and Gretel fattened up for the witch's spit. My own children are fearless. They put out candles with their fingers, dip them in hot candle wax. They light matches and hold onto them.

"Put away your childish things," I said, because we are leaving. "Save your favourites and give the rest away." Soon we'll be starting over.

Now, from my veiled vantage point, I wonder if that is wise. Is "moving on" a proper euphemism for slash and burn? Do I really expect to build our future on a cold fire? Will I wake up in my new bed in my new house with the taste of ashes in my mouth? Will they?

What are they doing in the garden? I should go out and ask. Some dead babies are buried there and several pets, even the rat that climbed the curtain. I hit it with a shovel, and the child who tried to kiss it goodbye before I stopped him buried it in a shoebox.

"Didn't you tell us we're all God's creatures? What about 'All my relations?'" My children are my conscience. Perhaps this is why they will inherit the Earth. Maybe they will take better care of it. I wonder if they are digging up the dead. "You said to take your favourites."

No sound from birds in their nests, sheep in the barn, only wind shivering trees, lifting a few loose shingles, soft socks on the stairs, up and down. The children are trying to be quiet.

Soon I will call them in from their night games, but not yet. It is after all the last time they will play in the garden. The moving truck is coming tomorrow morning.

Now when I try to remember sounds of life in this house, I only hear weeping.

Was that him? Did I miss something? The problem is, he was invisible too, except for the scent of lavender.

Now the sky lights up. Northern lights, perhaps, or lightning, a summer storm, but it isn't. I can see it clearly now. The light in the garden is the Child City, and it is burning.

MUD PIES

My maternal grandmother died the week I was born. I was travelling feet first, positioned to retrieve her Mrs. Beeton's Cookbook, every lady's guide to menu planning and servant management, while she flew first-class in the opposite direction. In my usual left-handed way, I failed to make the catch and entered the world empty-handed and crying out for custard.

An invalid, my grandmother must have spent most of her adult life eating comfort food. I must have inherited her addiction, bread highest on the list. Where else could it have come from?

I had the usual two grandmothers, one who lived and one who died. The one who died was from a rare breed, Austrian Jewish aristocrats too privileged for cooking but not immune to the ovens, where most of her cohort perished. Even if she hadn't been invalided by rheumatic fever, she would never have worn an apron.

The grandmother who lived was also visited by misfortune. My grandfather, the Seaforth Highlander who sang for the German and Canadian soldiers one Christmas in the trenches, became ill with tuberculosis after being gassed in France. Because he refused to die in the TB sanatorium, he had been allowed to come home on one condition, extreme hygiene. Cutlery was boiled. Tasting was verboten. That meant my surviving grandmother's kitchen was off limits.

Checkmate.

She did, however, give me her old clock when she replaced it with something turquoise and New Look during a fifties kitchen renovation. That clock, cream with big black deco letters, would get top dollar at a swap meet these days. She gave it to me for "playing house."

Kids don't play house. Kids do work. Whether it is over-watering a Wettums doll, covering sheets of paper with unintelligible child-glyphics or digging up the geraniums when I was asked to weed, I *worked* as hard as any adult.

Since my mother lacked a kitchen tradition, her Formica temple was as pristine as a layout for *House and Garden.* Singing, "mud, glorious mud," the Flanders and Swann song my father poured with bourbon over ice, I performed my cookery out of doors. In my summer kitchen, earth and sun facilitated the miracle of the loaves. I made the best dirt cuisine in the neighbourhood. Decorated with huckleberries, soapberries, rose and hydrangea petals, seasoned with love and solar energy, my mud pies were beautiful.

Crow, my Wettums doll, a shape changer, was the beneficiary of a new mother-to-daughter tradition. She never complained. The leftovers were for her. "Eat crow," my parents said, encouraging me to confess, and I confused them by eating Crow's fingers, you are what you eat, my mantra.

Bread is what mud pies aspire to be. These days, I am one of the world's leading bread-makers. The Queen of bread. Are my loaves uniform? No. I consider it a point of pride that after I won the Cowichan Fall Fair bread-making competition ten years in a row, they made a new rule, "that it had to fit in a toaster." What rubbish!

My bread becomes whatever it or I desire, a round, a square, a flower, a naked lady. When people ask what is in a loaf, I reply, "Look in the fridge." I may have leftover porridge, or chutney, or beer, or pesto sauce. Bread is life, and life is never the same.

However, in bread as in life and poetry, patience is essential. Meditation is the precursor to enlightenment. The brick-like doorjambs that often turn up at dinner parties are the result of rushing. Bread, like women in lust, should not be rushed.

My bread starts out with liquid at body temperature. That could be breast milk, beer, lemonade, mare's piss (filled with estrogen), whatever. To that liquid, I add an egg or eggs depending on how many I have. For a challah-type bread, up to a dozen eggs are mixed in. Sugar is important. That could be about a half cup of honey, sugar, molasses or jam to twoish cups of liquid.

The leavening agent is always yeast. I use about four tablespoons for fourish cups of flour and two cups liquid. The sugar and yeast should be dissolved before adding flour. The "ish" is important. We are feeling our way.

I add only half of the flour at the beginning to make what is euphemistically known as a sponge. Flour I stir in; and this is where poetry is important. A song, a poem, a significant number makes all the difference to the bread. The bread incantation is as vital as the one a mother chooses for childbirth. Think of the stirring as the labour. I enjoy the labour, knowing the results will be blissful.

Now the bread rises while I dance with a stray cat, read a magazine or go out for lunch. Like my husband, it waits for me.

When the sponge, covered by a damp tea towel, rises like the aforementioned lover, I add the rest of the flour, oil, salt, nuts, herbs, leftovers like porridge and beer, and knead. Kneading is what a cat does to get milk from its mother's breast. I fold the flesh over and over, do my age, which I won't reveal here. Suffice to say, it is enough.

Now it is time to read another magazine and let the dough rise. By the time the bread is cooked, I will know all the celebrity gossip. The mud rises at least twice, and I "punch" it each time. It helps to think of the Deranged Rooster or meter maids writing parking tickets. Rage is helpful, and no one charges bread-pummelers with assault. The kneading and rising processes stretch the gluten. There is time to make love between risings.

Several hours down the garden path, it is time for a final punch and the dividing of the loaves. I shape the dough and put on, or in, a well-oiled pan. I put herbs in the oil. They make a lovely crust. Sometimes I oil the whole loaf and cover it with rosemary (for remembrance), salt and garlic. A beaten egg makes a nice glaze, especially for a braided challah.

It is time to turn the oven on to 375 degrees. A pan of water left in the oven makes a "crustier" crust. That is a matter of choice. When the bread is fully risen, I put it in the oven and do the dance of joy a neighbour performs every time his grandchildren leave. After fifteen minutes, I turn the temperature down to 350 degrees. In an hour, when the top is golden and a rap on the crust produces a knock, the bread is ready. It will be a work of art. Trust the sponge method and me. We are infallible.

My real-life children were embarrassed about the oversized whole-wheat sandwiches in their lunch boxes. Everyone else at school had bologna on Wonder Bread. Wasn't it bad enough that they wore short pants and sandals in the redneck town where we sheep-farmed? Wasn't it bad enough that I put paintbrushes in their infant hands when all the other boys were given .22s for shooting rabbits and sometimes each other?

But that is jumping ahead. As it turned out, I was lucky to be married at all. My father had warned me numerous times that girls who dared to compete with boys usually lost out in the matrimonial market. I was a hopeless bluestocking, and the crème de menthe frappés my brother and I whipped up when our parents went to cocktail parties and charitable events were my only indoor kitchen skill.

The sidewalk where I laid out my mud pies was an altar. I had rituals—magical ingredients, a precise liturgy, incantations that ensured just the right amount of sunlight, and a worshipful congregation of kids who were awed by my infant poems and my baking.

However, there was one little boy, one devil with a buzz cut, who questioned my sacrament.

"It's just dirt," he said, poking my baking with a stick, threatening my doll.

"Bugger off, mean boy," I yelled, and a collective shiver told me the faithful were impressed with my syntax. In those days, kids got their mouths washed out with Dettol for using language like that. Their horror inspired me.

My grandmother's timepiece caught my eye. "Piss off, or I will clock you."

The crowd stood still. No one breathed. Stick Boy and I stood nose to nose in the ultimate game of boys against girls, which frequently ended in somebody taking down somebody else's underpants and revealing the secrets that inspired the mandatory separation of boys' and girls' washrooms.

I saw the pisspants bad boy's lip quiver. His eye twitched. He wanted to run home to his mother. I could tell.

"I dare you!" I said; the thrill shot an electrical current between my legs.

The crowd sighed and compressed as the neighbourhood fiend raised his omnipotent twig and came down with a splat on my lovely loaves.

"Ahhh!" If I had lit candles, they would have gone out. My pupils constricted. There was nothing left to do in the absence of light but retaliate. If I backed down, the feminist cause would be set back to the Dark Ages.

I lifted my grandmother's clock and brought it down on his head. The bad boy screamed; glass tinkled on the pavement. Blood gushed from his head.

Never run away from a wild animal, I remembered hearing on a scary radio show. I backed off, slowly retreated up the path, up the steps and through our front door.

My mother was busy not cooking. I ran past her, grabbed a pile of comic books and disappeared under my bed. My mother approached. All I could see were her feet in spectator shoes. She tapped her foot in an interrogatory pattern.

"What's up?"

"Nothing." My father was a lawyer. How many times had I heard him tell a client over the phone, "Say nothing?"

"Nothing?"

"That's right."

"Then what are you doing under your bed?"

"I just need a little time to myself."

"That's my line," she said.

"Yes," I replied. "That's right."

My mother returned to the living room, sat down and flipped through Eleanor Roosevelt's speech to the Appalachian coal miners. I could hear the pages slapping together, making almost as much noise as my panicked heart.

After an agony of waiting, justice knocked at our front door, and there was a sharp exchange. The door closed. My mother's spectator shoes made their way back to my bed and stood firm. I stopped breathing.

"So, you clocked the little bully down the street."

"Yes."

"He had eighteen stitches."

"Good," I said bravely.

"Yes," she said, "Good. Let's have cookies and milk."

She didn't spank me. That was for real crimes like sassing her back. I didn't have to do hard time, even though my mother thought it would be a wise idea to stay indoors for a couple of days, just for appearances.

I gave up on solar cooking, but the pleasure of mud never left me. On my birthday, my husband, who knows nothing about my proclivity for violence, took me to the Calistoga mud baths near his childhood home in Santa Rosa, California.

These days, I cook the way I write. I gather life's pleasure and some of its pain and dump it into a big mixing bowl. While I stir, I sing, recite, pray. The results are sometimes interesting. My husband calls my style "expressionist."

"What do you mean by that?" I ask.

He is a musician who plays from the heart. I hope he will say "heartfelt." He thinks for a moment, "Expressionism is an ordered chaos, a one-of-a-kind gestalt. Your cooking has order in that I can always guess what I am eating and chaos in that it is never the same."

I do not read instructions on packages. I do not read recipes. I will not be told how to think. I think that is a good thing. Surprise, some of my culinary results are stellar; and I am asked the inevitable question, "Can I have the recipe?"

What am I to say? Rilke said we must "live our way to the answers." Can my friends not live their ways to a heavenly soufflé (I am willing to say "Fresh eggs!") or an angelic loaf of bread ("Let it rise slowly."). When I taste something good, I close my eyes and accept it into my being. I learn music the same way. My husband, who is being much quoted in this piece and will probably experience a rush of ingratitude, says that playing music well is avoiding the wrong notes. Exactly. That is how to cook. Take risks, I say. Great art, great writing and great music don't come out the same way every time.

ONE MORE STORY

The child is watching. She's been here since sunrise, getting bolder by the hour. Now she is right in front of me.

"Why are you digging?"

"Looking for China."

"That's silly. I don't believe you. It would take forever."

What does she believe? Not in the tooth fairy or Santa Claus. This is a practical girl with a handsome, almost adult, face she will grow into. Oh how I wish for an after-life that will allow me to witness this lovely child as an adult, going about the world dispensing kindness as she does now, taking her drawings, her homemade cookies and healing touch to the street and the rest home where her elder-friends are incarcertated. Stay kind, I say, when her little fists clench, when the world of television news assaults her. Turn the other cheek, but stay standing.

"Forever is for fairy tales."

I have to blow her off with brevity. There's no time to dispute the nature of being with an argumentative primary schooler. Digging is not an exact science, but I do need to concentrate.

How many times have I said, Watch me, just as I did with her father, who has turned out to be a good father, a good cook, a reader and a good gardener, his male and female in balance. Write things down if you like, then chew up the paper and swallow. These are adaptable truths, my recipes. I tell her recipes evolve, change like crows imitating voices.

I have changed, left fear behind, and that is a blessing. I think she is already fearless.

There was a time when I believed my soufflés would fall and my words would fail if I let go of my rituals. When I whipped eggs or stirred the sponge for my bread, I would beat my age, no more, no less.

Then there were other lists, for a while my phobias, a family joke. I went from ablutophobia to zoophobia and back. You're wearing out the flour, they told me, stretching your gluten to the moon. It was true. I agreed my crusts were tough and my arms worn out, and I quit baking and knitting cold turkey, consoling myself with old movies and buckets of gin. My rituals are no longer about fear. They are simply parameters.

"How many scoops in a bucket?" she asks.

"I'm not counting," I say.

She's laughing. They all laugh. Come on. I may be neurotic, but I am not stupid.

"That's rude."

They've noticed I'm anxious in a new way, can't wait for the green bananas and long-playing records. My embedded rituals are, as ever, comforting: the tea at four with the spoon in the four o'clock position ritual, the eighty-six attacks on my tooth enamel and my thinning hair rituals. Damn, I'm going to be tidy when I meet my holy bridegroom.

Now I'm a digger, no, *not* a not Protestant anarchist, but Voltaire's disciple, God's gardener digging to China, twenty scoops in a bucket, eighty-seven buckets, a bed. I love dirt. It is not dirty, not anymore. Now it is *terroir,* that beautiful word, *stars* fueling up for my backwards ride to the firmament, no longer the septic host to pernicious microbes. Now I fancy myself falling asleep in my luxurious dirt bath on the other side of the forest, future food for a vintage wine or everbearing strawberry, grass for hungry goats.

I'm a small woman, slowly shrinking from formidable to adorable, now an apple doll of a person, something to cuddle rather than confront, going for a finite number. When I get to magic eighty-seven, the hole should be big enough, every load marked with my stick, just in case I forget, which is becoming all too common.

I can't remember the first word I misplaced, so I'll go through the alphabet, all the way to polyanthus, then porcine—it can't be phobia. Phobia is unforgettable, greasy movie hotdogs, sounds like throat boogers, the gob of anxiety, the one that gives people cancer and sclerotic arteries, the noun that keeps us alert. I miss my nouns. Sometimes I lie awake at night, naming things. How much longer will I remember them? That is the cruellest question.

Phobias have been my little helpers, elves and fairies. Once upon a time, I knew the word for every one. I wrote them on Post-its, tacked them on my wall. Choose one and write a story, I said to myself. Draw a picture. Anxiety is helpful to artists, manifests in notes that push away fear, splashes of colour that frighten the devil and all his accomplices, spells that summon the angels protecting us.

"Do you know the word for "fear of dirt"?" I decide to engage her, *a little.* We love to play dictionary, and she consumes words like a hungry puppy, but, although generous in other ways, she doles them out carefully as if she were in a child court of law, as if everything depended on thrift. Sometimes I worry the rest of the family talks so much there is no room for her, but she makes her own spaces. When she speaks, it matters.

"You said it was *meso* something."

"*Mysophobia.* I'm over that one."

"We made mud pies, remember, when I got upset about dirt."

"And now you're a real outdoor girl. Was that you spying on me yesterday while I was staking my bed? I thought I saw your yellow dress in the trees."

"That was me."

"I," I say.

Goddamn. My bad. Rule number one, thou shalt only correct a child's grammar indirectly, by example.

"Sorry."

"Whatever."

"Double sorry with sugar on top."

"I'll forgive you if you tell me a story."

"OK. After this bucket." Today she is wearing shorts and sandals. In the sixties, I sent my boys to primary school in shorts and sandals, with girl-shirts and bowl haircuts. They still haven't forgiven me.

"Nothing wrong with being a hippy," I think out loud.

"What's that?"

"Never mind."

"Hippos are nearly extinct. So are pandas, polar bears and pygmy elephants."

I put down my trowel and sit on the edge of the hole. "You're a smart girl. Do you know what a zoophobe is?"

"Someone who hates zoos. I hate zoos. They shouldn't lock animals up."

"You are right and not quite right. Zoophobes are people who fear animals."

"I'm not afraid of any, any animal, not even wasps. They only sting you if you pester them." She sits beside me, throws a handful back in, the tease.

"I wasn't always afraid. I didn't want anything to hurt my babies. It wasn't about me." That was when I started drinking, I said to myself, but not to her. Too much information. She wouldn't remember that.

"I'm all about me," she says.

"That's normal for your age, six, right?"

"No, seven." This is our inside joke. I keep telling her not to grow up too fast.

"I'm almost eighty-seven."

"I know. Tomorrow's your birthday."

Gerontophobia, fear of growing old. I didn't have that one. That was gravity, the way to this very moment.

"What are you afraid of, Geegee?"

"Nothing now. Not a damn thing."

"What about people afraid of people?"

"That's the big one, the worst one of all."

"I'm not afraid."

"Me either."

"Neither."

"Whatever. I'm almost done. I'm closing in on the magic number."

"What's that?"

"It doesn't matter. I'm just done with worrying." I survey the mound of dirt beside the hole and the hole itself, a single bed as it were, just enough room to lie back and enjoy the night sky, and a few sips. I brought my down pillow.

"Have you ever tasted champagne?"

"No, but I'd like to."

"I only have one mug."

"We can share."

"You bet we can. We're from the same germ bed." The first time I told her that was when she asked if it was safe to kiss me on the lips.

"Is this kind of a sleepover?"

"You could say that."

"I like sleepovers."

"Then I will tell you a scary sleepover story."

“I like scary.” This is new. Usually, she gets to choose between scary, funny and wonderland, and she has never chosen scary. She waits for me to start.

“Once upon a time, a man and wife were on their honeymoon on the *Playa del Este* in Cuba. *Playa del Este* means eastern beach, where easterly winds make enormous waves in the sea and blow the sand around.

“The husband loved his wife dearly, and kept touching their wedding rings because he couldn’t believe his luck in finding a bride and hopefully a mother for his children.

“He would do anything for her, anything but swimming. He couldn’t go in the ocean with her, because he was aquaphobic, afraid of the water and sea creatures ever since he had a dream about drowning.

“His wife thought that was silly. She was a ballerina in the water, so of course she went swimming without him while he sat under an umbrella and watched her perform her water wheels and oysters.

“I know what those are.”

“Of course you do. You are poetry in the pool.”

“After only a few minutes, out of the blue, the sun disappeared behind dark clouds stirred up by easterly winds. That was some storm. The groom called his new wife in from the sea, and she swam back to the beach where he waited with his mind in an anxious knot.

“He grabbed her cold hand, recently given to him in marriage, pulled her close, so she could feel his heart pounding and felt her wedding finger, the one joined by blood to her feelings.

"There was nothing there but skin and bone.

"Where's your ring?" he cried, and she felt its absence, then fell to pieces.

"My ring's gone. I've lost it!"

"Together, the new husband and wife searched the shoreline. She apologized over and over. It was her fault for so many reasons. She was showing off. She was teasing him. She wasn't going to wear a wife collar and leash and be led. They looked frantically, clawing the sand and seaweed, and found fish bones, shells, a plastic bucket and a child's shovel, but no wedding ring.

"They were student volunteers who'd come to Cuba after the revolution to build a clinic and had saved up for their wedding bands."

"It must be in the ocean," she said, weeping, her storm almost as big as the one tearing up the sea and disturbing the sand on the beach.

"This was not a good omen. He was terrified, but he had to show her he was brave enough to save their marriage. She didn't have time to say, 'Don't be silly. Forever is more than a ring.'"

"I'm going in." He grabbed her goggles and plunged into the water.

"The lifeguard ran down the beach. '*Mal agua,*' he shouted, '*Mal agua.*'

"Neither husband nor wife spoke Spanish well. They thought *mal agua* meant bad water, a storm with big waves. That was obvious. How could they know *mal agua* meant this wind brought bad water *and* poisonous jellyfish?

"The bridegroom remembered how to swim from the time before the terrible dream he hadn't explained in full detail. All he'd said was, 'I am afraid to go in the water.' He walked into the sea and swam out to the place where she had gone back and forth, teasing him with her water ballet.

"She watched him dive, her heart smashing against waves of fear. Down he went, and up. The lifeguard stood helpless at the shore. He'd warned them, hadn't signed up for this gringo foolishness. The lifeguard had a family to support.

"Down the bridegroom went, and stayed there.

"I can't see him," the bride screamed and paced, counting the seconds. It has to be a joke. He'll come back. "*Mal agua,*" the lifeguard kept saying, and still he didn't go in after the foundering groom.

"Some times take forever.

"After forever, a wave delivered her oyster blue bridegroom with her ring on his baby finger and jellyfish stings swelling all over his body.

"This must have been the dream he had before he stopped swimming, the part he hadn't mentioned.

"Is that a true story?" the child asks.

"Yes, or I wouldn't have told you."

I left out the part about the bride being already pregnant, with twins.

"It isn't nice to scare little girls."

"But you said you weren't scared of anything."

"I'm only *not* afraid of make believe things."

"Sometimes there are reasons for frightening kids. It keeps them safe."

"Oh sure, I get it about crossing the street and drinking poison, but what about war and climate change? How would scaring kids about stuff like that help us?"

"Because kids imagine, and someone has to think up ways to fix the terrible mistakes that adults make. Someone has to find the cures for war and disease and pollution, for greed."

I get back to scooping dirt in my bucket. Now I'm at sixty-seven.

"Seven is my lucky number. You should stop at seventy-seven."

"It's too late for that. It's time to go home."

"I'm not leaving until you do."

"Eventually, you will have to go back to the house. Soon it will be dinnertime, and you will be hungry. You will have to leave me here and go through the woods like Little Red Riding Hood. Just go before dark and stay on the path."

Soon the sun will disappear behind the trees. Her legs are bare, I can see the fine hairs on her baby girl shins and arms are rigid with cold.

The trowel holds about a cup. It is comforting to measure out the dirt that will cover my grave, just like cooking. I know the basic chemistry, so much flour to so much yeast or baking powder, so much oil, so many eggs and cups of liquid, plus the serendipitous, whatever walks into my head or out of my refrigerator. Once I knew that; I knew it all. Now I know the Socratic nothing.

I cook the way I do everything: my garden rambles, my meals surprise, my poems assault. There is no fixed recipe for life.

"Let's go home and make a birthday cake," the child is shivering.

"It's your turn. You go make it all by yourself."

"I like doing it together."

"When you are older, remember to read the philosopher Bishop Berkeley. He will tell you anything you imagine is real. Just imagine I am there when I'm not."

"Can we open the bottle now?" These scary abstractions are not for her, not now.

"One more bucket." I slow down, watching the child, memorizing every detail. I've heard it is possible to take telegrams to the dead. What message would he want from his children, grandchildren and great-grandchild?

I already know. He will want to know that they are kind. That is all.

I hope I will still recognize him. It has been so many years, three generations. Will he be the same? Will I? Will he recoil at the lustful bag of wrinkles and brown spots chasing him down those streets paved with gold?

"Why are you laughing?"

"I'm laughing at myself. It's a great trick. If you can flip every bad thing into a lesson or some kind of joke, then you will get through everything life throws at you. It works for me."

"I try to laugh when I muck things up."

"That's the spirit."

"Open the bottle." She hands it to me, maybe expecting I will open it the way I have popped the cork on many bottles of plonk, banging the heel against a door frame. This is one of my party tricks.

There is a portal here, and it isn't the cuneiform shape I have dug, wide at one end so I can move my wings. It is blue sky. I wonder if I should tell our beautiful girl about the etymology of the word "cunt," birth and death, or is that too complicated? Will the child's parents be angry about my ultimate pedagogy? I have been found guilty before, guilty of giving her candy, buying her Spanish dance shoes with taps and high heels, makeup.

Girls should know that "cunt" is a good word.

"Stand back," I say. I remove the foil and pop the cork. She stands her ground, and it goes right in her eye. She will have a shiner. Not the end of the world. She smiles, shows her big new teeth. "I'll have a trophy." Yes, she gets it. I took her to the roller derby, where bruises are trophies.

I pour the bubbly into the tin cup. "*Prosit*," I say. She says, "*Mazeltov.*" I say, "*Salute.*" "*Slainte.*" "*Meegwech.*" All my relations. She has the first sip. I have the second. We pour some in the ground.

"I'm going to rest now," I say, putting my down pillow down in the dirt, avoiding the word "sleep." She knows the word "hypnophobia." I'm over that too.

"I'm cold. Can I lie with you?"

"Only until I am cold. Then you must go home."

She climbs down and snuggles. "Is that what we're playing, hot and cold?"

We play the game on our birthdays, hers, mine, and her parents. The closer we get to the hidden gift, the hotter it gets. We chant in unison. It is almost my last birthday, time to leave the greatest gift behind. Her.

"Hotter is home. You go there. Your parents will need you."

Clever little girl, she gets it. "Tell me one more story," she says, "and I will go. I promise.

MR. AND MRS. SMITH

Jane and her twin sister Janet think of their dolls as left and right identical, made from a pair of war-rationed stockings. Along with sugar and eggs, their Scottish aunts, also identical twins, were allowed one pair of stockings each coupon period.

From this rare extravagance, the aunts sewed perfect dolls: no runs, no tears, gifts as generous as the precious books that came every Christmas without fail and erased the degree of separation between Scotland and Canada, aunts and grand-nieces, war and peace. Reality and fiction.

The twins' Scottish ancestors were Vikings, red-haired, hot-tempered, difficult to anaesthetize. The only black person their family knew intimately was their housekeeper, Virginia, with them, their father explained, to replace their mother who had "gone barking," which meant "singing" (and maybe "fucking") on the stages of the world.

Virginia, who polished with lemon oil and drank lemon water by the quart, smelled like lemons. Their mother, who rode horses when she wasn't warning the world, smelled like horses. Piss straw, manure, leather and lather, animal sweat.

Mr. and Mrs. Smith had no genitals. They were made from the chocolate-coloured ration stockings, and with black woolly hair and button eyes, looked exactly the same, except one had a violet wool dress with a scalloped hem and the other wore violet wool pants, both reversible, with moss green on the inside.

Given that their mother was away most of the time, the Smith dolls saw the girls through every childhood illness: measles, mumps, chicken pox, parental dysfunction and influenza. "Influenza" means "against the stars," and that was how they thought of their mother.

Virginia said their mother was "doing good work," breaking glasses and glass ceilings using her fame to campaign for feminism and social justice. At home, out of the public eye, she broke things that belonged to their father and flushed his rye down the toilet, incidents Virginia called "collateral damage."

Wish I had a plane to fly.
Here's what I'd write in the sky,
Gone fishin' instead of just a wishin'

When Virginia, saint of their troubled household, went home to her own family, their mother tore the house apart looking for irregularities: smudges on the woodwork (a theme reprised in Tea Party lamentation about the condition of the White House during Obama's term of office), dust on the ledges and traces of fat in the oven.

"Lazy black bitch," she said, clearly, no doubt about the diction of Our Lady of Dog Notes, coloratura champ.

At the end of her second pregnancy, Virginia sat down a lot, polishing silver. That was way past lazy. Their mother said it the way she said "beyond the pale."

"We're all survivors of something," Virginia said, possibly hearing oars plodding across the Atlantic Ocean, against the current. Several times a day, she took a photo of her infant daughters out of her pocket and kissed it.

Their mother had "hard hands," their father said, which meant she rode people hard. Jane and Janet wondered if there was ever a time when their father enjoyed that, but never asked.

The Smiths loved Virginia, and the twins did too. In the beginning, she sang them to sleep, their dolls cradled in their arms, then dressed up for dance dates with her husband, a porter who rode the trains. That was in the beginning. Later as she transformed from awesomely bright, tight satin dresses, high heels, purple eye shadow, into a grey chrysalis, she went off to Bible classes.

Virginia was awesome, her cooking was awesome, her kindness was awesome. She made the trade, lost her bebop and found her gospel bounce, but her heart stayed rainbow brilliant. Virginia was saved, baptized in the Baptist church, as her lullabies moved on from "I'm Your Hoochie Coochie Man" and "Boom, Boom, Boom" to "How Awesome Is My God." She washed off her makeup and giddiness in the blood of the Lamb, but inside her renovated façade, her bones danced on.

The thrill was gone, but not the beat.

The Smiths also bounced. In the dark, empowered by music, their silent best friends rose up from doll paralysis, jumping and jiving on their beds, saved by the Lord. Sometimes making babies. The twins practised too, clothes on.

In the morning, no dark smudges marred their sheets, and in one of those moments when children realise their parents are not exactly what they hoped they might be, Jane understood that the fingerprints on the woodwork belonged to white folks. That would be their father, their mother, Janet and her.

So much for golliwogs. What did they know? The Smiths were their morning and evening stars.

Postcards from New York, London, San Francisco and Paris marked their passage through illness and honour rolls. They kept on sucking their thumbs until they needed to act like grown-ups. All along they had tried on their mother's clothes when she was away, inhabiting their idea of her.

When they turned twelve, the dress with fringes their mother brought home from her nights at Studio 54 actually fit them. Janet, who had more of a waist, wore the black velvet with a pink silk rose on the bosom. They stood in front of the floor-length mirror and shook what Virginia, back in her juke days, called their moneymakers.

When their mother came home, she raged. Something

was awry in her closet. Her wardrobe was colour-coded and carefully aligned, shoe-to-shoe, dress-to-dress. "Someone's been wearing my shoes," she said, surprising the hell out of them with her knowledge of childhood fairy tales, something she had neglected to share.

Later, after a Librium and the speed that kept her skinny, she said in her sotto voce telephone voice, "You've been up to something." Usually, she noticed minutiae, but not big picture things. That came later, when Janet surprised her with a left hook to the jaw that knocked her out cold.

The family silver shone, and there were more fingerprints. Virginia, pregnant for the third time, was sacked.

Who would the twins sing and dance with? Who would hold back the shadows at night? Who would put her cool hand on their feverish foreheads and keep their hair out of the way when they were sick without leaving a single fingerprint?

The girls held onto their dolls, also grieving, for dear life. There were no more backflips, no tumbling on their beds, but at least Mr. and Mrs. Smith were there with their eyes wide open, taking everything in.

"We can see you," Janet hissed from the top bunk when their mother made a surprise bedroom visit and got into bed with Jane. She had been fast asleep, maybe dreaming, and woke up holding her breath, wondering what came next, a fairy tale, a tune? She had no songs to sing, just a secret she was going to keep.

Where was Dad, she panicked? Probably Dad was in

his usual place, his face in a book, Puccini screaming on the gramophone, the Mills Brothers.

"I'm going to buy a paper doll that I can call my own," the Mills Brothers crooned on the record player. Their father told them the Mills Brothers were staying at his friend's house because the hotel where they were performing wouldn't have black men in their rooms. Oh yes, they thought, smudge marks on the sheets and woodwork, big black rings on the bathtub.

"Leave her alone," Janet said, and their mother turned the Smith faces to the wall.

The aunts had not sewn ears on the Smiths. Not that dolls with ears listen anyway.

"I like girls," their mother said.

"Me too," Jane answered. She liked Virginia and her sister. They were her world.

"I mean, beyond like. I like to touch them." She gathered the dolls and took off their clothing. "See," she said, pointing to their identical gender spots, clefts stitched in wool the same colour as the stockings so she could barely see them.

Both girls. The bowling team, friends of Dorothy's, unfamiliar phrases whizzed by. It was some joke the Scottish aunts were in on. Jane was not in the club. Janet said she was not in the club either. They didn't want to be in the club. It was the club that took mothers away from daughters and turned their fathers into drunks.

When their mother left their room, Janet jumped into bed with Jane, and they rubbed the undressed Smiths together until their sock bodies ripped and their stuffing fell out. “Like, like, like,” they whispered, furious, as if young girls with flammable skirts and cloth dolls were fire starter, embers that stoked aberrant mothers.

Of course, full realisation came slowly, over the years it took the Smiths to rot in the graveyard behind their house, under the star magnolia where their canaries slept in cardboard coffins.

Jane stole bread and ate it under the covers, handfuls of soft dough. She sucked her thumb. Janet masturbated noisily under her blankets. It was all about hunger, and they knew. It is worse to know and do nothing.

The Smiths had a terrible death. The twins made a bonfire of all the books from the aunts and lay their golliwogs on top. They didn’t know who was up, Mr. or Mrs. Smith, because naked they were identical. They faced each other, top and bottom like the bunk bed.

The Smiths burned slowly, and Janet used the poker to move them further into the fire. Burn baby burn.

They heard them scream.

Then it rained, and they dug a hole for their charred remains under the star magnolia tree, beside the dead pets.

The Smiths died like Adam and Eve or Adam and Adam, Eve and Eve, naked, expelled from the garden, half-baked in a paper fire. Genesis, Exodus, the same old story.

Jane keeps the Smith clothes in a small cedar box. Sometimes she opens it up and sniffs. They smell like Virginia. Nice. Not like horses.

HER NAME

It's the scent. Tonight the forest leaking through the open windows smells like earth, a compost cake, vegan, lemons and nuts squeezed in her pristine colon, but she's getting ahead of herself, in the way, as usual, of the answers. First, the question, why has her life been twisted, an explanation mark with scoliosis?

After saying goodnight to her TV, she makes a violent pivot, splashes down her cup of milk, throws open the door to the garden and breathes in the night: ocean, wisteria, with frog jism the dominant note because the frogs are singing, spitting out spring lust, and the crows harmonize, a fifth apart.

Their singing pulls her into the darkness, across the damp lawn, moss, to the forest floor.

She's left the door open for home invaders, rats, squirrels, predators. This is new style: the open door, welcome. She's been waiting in the locked house for the next thing to happen, the assumption being she'd always get to ride in the bitch position behind a dark rider. All her life she's avoided surprises, but maybe there's a good one around the next corner or reaching out of a crack in the pavement.

She's in her pyjamas. Without thinking, even of putting on shoes or a sweater, she slips through the relaxed portal into moonlight, fearful to fearless. Found in translation; what does it mean when stars hanging like lamps in the sky wait for sunrise that happens, then disappears, either over the horizon or into the eternal greyness of days turning on and off like electric lights?

Dreaming through fog, clouds on the ground, running with sex feelings sharing the same primal space, she trips on a root, grabs at crumbling bark, moss, dirt, drops her glasses, pulls herself up, takes a breath and squints back at the house, the open door and the unblinking second-floor bedroom windows, three pairs of animal eyes, all feral, hungry, the odd triplet: Father, Mother, Daughter, beaming light on the grass and beyond.

Who switches on the lights in their bedrooms when no one is home? Not her mother. Not her father, who sent her typewritten letters from prison, then disappeared.

She's in the woods on all fours; sniffing hands caked with dirt, hoping she won't step on her specs. How to translate dirt, *terroir,* into mushroom, wine, words that feed a soul insatiably hungry, hoping to open the doors to unexpected surprises, or familiar reassurance, rooms filled with old furniture and new prospects: food she has never tasted, views she could possibly replicate if she could just get it right?

On the other side of the door, the subconscious, Magritte's reversible dream, a surreal life, the dream translated, life turned inside out. She could be a sleepwalker, bumping into familiar things in the dark, sometimes her parents one after the other, never quite understanding what or why.

Isn't that a mother's job, orchestrating sound walks into real life outside the submersible womb? Her own was no spirit guide, never took her by the hand and led her while simultaneously reciting family recipes for shortbread and chutney and the thou-shalt-nots: shalt not cross her eyes or leave her shoes unlaced, protect Daddy when he translates crystal caves into scary moments, and after exile, sends surrogates to peer in her window at night, tapping on the glass with filthy fingernails.

It's a staring game, eyes glittering in the forest, windows staring into the darkness, her parents playing chicken in court. Then, she took off her glasses so she wouldn't have to have eye contact with either one of them.

Now she looks up and sees them, caught on a branch, gleaming in the moonlight. She puts them back on. Focus. Unfocus. Her crystal balls. She got her bad eyesight from someone who typed with his nose on the keyboard, lost his way in the house at night, was pulled to her light like a deranged moth with pockets full of articulate crystals. "Choose your story: snowflake, sugar, pillar of salt."

So she chose, and he mapped the plot with his magic fingers, touch-typing.

She actually feels safer outdoors. These woods filled with the dark shapes of evergreen and branches with spiderwebs waiting to trap her are not nearly as scary as the shadows in the house, arrested typing, footsteps on the stairs, her unlocking simply defiance: of herself, of memory, a dead man walking.

While her eyes adjust to her glasses, she glances around and sees, what is it called, pareidolia, familiar faces all around her. Face actually, her father's visage carved in every tree trunk, his mouth open wide, a scream. She's not afraid. They are in the same lonely club, tapping keys, listening for the great design that will lift them up.

A little night music, the sound of her bare feet in the damp forest floor, the sound of moonlight forcing itself through cracks in leaves that catch tears from heaven.

She buried her dog here, on the edge, where the wild rhododendrons and blackberries seeded themselves. Soleil, her golden lab, daughter of Luna who led her mother to the infant buried in the woods, died of a heart attack the night of the Storm this February. The dog went out to pee and never came back. It was snowing, and she waited in the house, never thinking the worst had happened. Soleil had scratched at the door. She wanted out. Trees were falling. Shakes flew off the roof.

The young bitch died of a heart attack, and when she went to look for her in the first light of morning, she only had to follow her cat's footprints. When she got there, the cat, Diablo, black as night, was keening, licking Soleil's ears.

The rhododendrons bloomed early this year, bright pink, pinker than usual, nourished by the blood of her dear companion. She's heard stories like this about the poppies thriving on blood spilled in battlegrounds, Flanders Fields.

Tonight is the first time she's penetrated the forest devastation. In the dark, her song line is different, the familiar no longer the map she memorised when she was a child, steps she could have taken blindfolded: here is my arbutus with bear scratches, here is my first fort, and here are the ferns I used to sweep my forts. Here is my loo. Here are my huckleberries. Here are my salmonberries. Here is my summer kitchen.

Here is where I hid from my parents.

Tonight, the trees and bushes frame unfamiliar rooms. Next fall, she will rent a chainsaw, clear the brush and cut up firewood.

Her father had a passion for firewood. Every year he cut far more than they could burn. His pile might have covered a parking lot. It was his tension relief, one of several, the others being whiskey, typing letters and misplaced affection. He would chop and chop, and people thought it was funny because his day job was surgery, "Get it out of your system," his friends laughed. "Better to chop up wood than your patients." He was a neurosurgeon, and he had operated on the Pope to cure his hiccoughs, but skilled as he was with a knife, he could not cut his way out of jail.

After they took him away, she and her mother kept burning the chopped wood and never attempted to replace it. This new windfall will be the second lot in years, almost a quarter century.

It might be her imagination or a woodpecker deranged by head banging, pecking insect holes in a tree, but she thinks she hears hammers attacking the dead wood. These are the ghosts she lives with; percussive noises: footsteps in the hall, typewriter keys, woodpeckers, the piano. When she can't stand it, she wears buds in her ears.

Now she is almost naked in the shivery night: no shoes, no jacket and no plugs. She does have her glasses, lucky her, hears with her eyes and her ears, maybe a cougar breathing hard, wondering if he should dance with her in the moonlight, perhaps a wild woman heavy with stolen children, or just wind in the leaves.

When Luna dug up the corpse, she brought it home as she had been trained to do. Luna was a swimmer who would jump into the coldest lake to retrieve a bird, and a digger who regularly unearthed treasure, sometimes carrots from the garden and sometimes candies buried by squirrels. This time it was the little blue non-person no one had noticed growing under man-shirts she'd borrowed from her dad.

She'd wished it out early, huffed and puffed and jumped on her trampoline, then had violent cramps in the woods, and it came out fast. The slippery thing was dead already, not ready, one of those silences whose trajectory is a tunnel of darkness. She buried it and went into the house in time for dinner, her hem wet with blood and amniotic fluid, her delta aching.

Days later, she was at the library looking up books on semiotics. Her mother was writing a speech, her left hand dragging ink across the paper. Her father was drinking, typing on his Olivetti in the library, home from one of his covert operations, cutting into the brain of a deranged dictator, getting rid of a tic. Luna, moon dog, delivered the package wrapped in her sweater, dropped it under the dining room table, a little surprise, something for the dysfunctional family dinner.

Her mother saw it first. She knew right away. It had the giveaway father-and-daughter halo. Ginger. When she came home with her load of borrowed books, the police were already there.

"It isn't what you think," she said, her famous last words, before they could say what they thought. She has always had the gift, or curse, of premonition.

So she slammed her door. Shut up.

Tonight, she feels him close in the woods, his breath in her ear the one sound she can't block out. She calls it tinnitus, but what does she know? It is just a voice. Voices. She can't recall her mother's voice. That was probably because she had so many: the corporate voice, the commanding feminist voice, the good cop voice luring her to the priest, confession, the metal voice that critiqued everything from her table manners to her appearance, the contemptuous voice for her father and the seductive voice on the phone, when she'd caught her touching herself. No. Not caught, startled her while...

Now, the disingenuous stranger on her answering machine says, "Stop texting. Your mother doesn't like it."

"The Stranger" is a character who apparently appeared out of red smog with a guitar and a knapsack full of fiction.

Women made her suspicious of women, and her father, sick as he was, the healer, of men, but he also gave her a love of precise language. His voice, she remembers.

Luna had a baby too. She died in childbirth with seven other pups, but Soleil survived, and she fed her milk in a doll bottle. No one spoke but the dog, who barked when she wanted in and out and when she was hungry, and not so long after, her mother packed her bags and silently left. Her mother's lawyer sent her the title to the house and notice that money would be put in her bank account at the beginning of every month. A handwritten insert said, "Don't look for me," but she did, and that was more or less a dead end that led to the stranger, the voice on the phone. No point sending the dog after her. She would only kick her.

Her father took his typewriter to prison. Every week, she got a note, always the same, always different. The different part was a list of books she should read, and the semblable was the ending, "I'm sorry." She read the books, mostly about miracles like parthenogenesis and binary fission, and wondered when and if he would tell her more. What was it like in jail? Did he crawl into someone's bunk and tell his wonderful stories? Did they let him heal? He was a good healer. She never wrote back, just assumed the connection. Never asked why he did it, because she knew. It was all about crystals, a phenomenon her mother didn't get. Her mother was an inscrutable crystal, salt in their wound.

Then the letters stopped. He stopped. Maybe his inappropriate affection curdled. Maybe he was no longer sorry. Maybe he got out and got lost. Maybe his sorrow and loneliness turned into cancer and choked him. Perhaps another prisoner shivved him with an improvised knife—a chopstick or a pencil—or put an eggbeater up his rectum. These things happen in jail, especially to the child abuser; understandable, most prisoners having been abused as children. Maybe he knotted his sheets and pillow slip together and hung himself in his cell, like Hernandez, the sociopath wide end receiver who later turned out to have Spam brain from head bumps.

It also occurred to her that, if he were alive, he might come back to find her, his cosmic twin. She had nothing to say, no words of forgiveness or recrimination, kept the windows and doors locked. When she graduated from university, the mailman delivered an anonymous gift. It was a necklace with typewriter letters spelling her name.

She had a stalker at the time, someone with black curly hair who worked at the library and put love letters in the books she borrowed. She assumed it was him. No reason not to. He brought stolen flowers every week, little dandelion and wild lupin posies she found on the doormat.

She is an anomaly, attracting aberration, a crystallographic defect, rogue molecules desiring nothing but symmetry. She answers the dark, thinking out loud, the Bjork lyrics.

Crystals grow like plants (listen how they grow)
I'm blinded by the lights (listen how they glow)
In the core of the earth (listen how they grow)

She hears them all, the rocks, the diamonds, Bjork in swan feathers at the Oscars, her father's stories, her mother's excuses. She and her father were that anomaly, twinned pyrite, their asexual reproduction binary fission energised by the telling of stories, romance, the tickle that scared her, not because of its deviance but because of its overwhelming magnificence.

How could she tell that to the cops? Cops are blunt, insensitive to the nuance of narrative arc, two anomalies bending the rainbow. How could she tell her mother, who was into man blaming, and impervious to her reasoning?

The stone forest floor is trembling. She can feel it now, the truth coming out, rock tremours cracking the Earth, crow watching, the tapping noise getting closer. Her father taught her about aboriginal sound walks, sonar navigation, useful when the night sky clouds over. But this is not a dark night. The stars are speaking too, music crackling on wires strung from black hole to black hole. Who to believe? Look up. Look down.

In that order. She has done it. Looking up, she sees the lamps blinking though cracks in the forest. And a cedar brought down, likely uprooted by the storm that scared her dog to death. And a hole, what little kids call a hidey-hole, just enough room for a child who has been terrified by adult behaviour to curl up and sleep.

She runs her hand along the peeling, bleeding bark. This could be the bloody crucifix in the resurrection story. If she licks her hand, she will taste blood. She knows what that tastes like. She has eaten her own scabs. She tasted the blood that came out with the child and stained her hem.

The tree cavity feels and smells like a cave with earth walls. She tries to crawl in, but can't. It is not big enough for a thirty-nine-year-old woman. There is something hard in there. She digs around the thing and frees it, pulls it out.

It is a small dirt-smeared suitcase with a broken handle and rusty hinges, just large enough for a baby or a cat. She has buried dead things in these woods and doesn't want to open it. Fear or sacrilege? Whatever, she is afraid, so she sits with the coffin box in the moonlight, not quite grieving like mourners who sit up all night with the corpses of their beloved, but like a witness not quite sure of what she's witnessing.

Eventually the sun rises as usual, at civic twilight, her most difficult time, the hour between haunted nights and enigmatic mornings. She will either leave the suitcase and return to the house or she will open it up and learn something she may or may not want to know. There might be money inside, thousands or millions of dollars stashed by a mattress millionaire or a bank robber, one of her father's new friends. Maybe he was the one who clawed her windows at night looking for a safe place to hide, having been assured by his cellmate of her vulnerability to story.

There is no key, but the latch leaps open when she touches it.

Inside is a typewriter. She recognises the green Olivetti, its carriage cover replaced by what she recognizes as prison issue, a plastic cover so that contraband could not be hidden there. And what she sees is that the type slugs on the ends of the hammers have been cut out. Like her tongue, she thinks. A large crystal, an amethyst as big as a child's fist, nestles in the gap. The typewriter is bound with barbed wire, and inside this perverse ribbon, a wound wound, are photos of her, now and then in the garden, and a letter wrapped in a plastic bag.

It says sorry, sorry, sorry, sorry, over and over. Just "sorry," a word, a sutra, that moves as slowly as a river, her bloodstream, the time apart from herself, whatever that is. Sorry, a wound bound in typewriter ribbon, and healing, a surgeon's beautiful stitchery, the blessing of moving water, self-absolving rivers anointing the dead and the living. It just keeps on moving, the penultimate vowel almost the end, but the end never comes. Sorry...

Some keys are missing.

The letters that spell her name are missing in action. If she waits, still and silent, listening, she might hear the slugs sliding on iridescent carpets of slime, over the forest floor, toward her. They will say her name. And she might answer.

WOOLGATHERER

Usually, especially on warm afternoons, she falls asleep counting sheep, the drowsy clouds, *nuages*, such beautiful words for molecules of water suspended in air, *nubo* in Esperanto, baby shoes about to drop, precipitation, lovely consonants, lovely diction, the beat.

"Are you deaf or stupid," is the louche question people keep asking, and she answers, moving her lips but not making a sound, making the louche questioners read, as she must, "I am deaf, and you are thick as fog, thicker than cardboard, deeply, deeply stupid." Unkind stupid is the worst kind.

Her sleepy tongue embraces the new inconsonance.

Woolgathering. Her mother encouraged it, gave her every opportunity to consort with fluff. Grace grew up on a sheep farm. She was the gatherer, the child who went to the henhouse thrumming with *berk, berk, berk* before breakfast and thrust her hand under cosy hen-breasts to collect the eggs, the one who picked watercress from the stream that ran through the orchard, the wild asparagus that grew beside the river and tasted of tides, and the tufts left behind on thistles and barbed wire fences, wool she used to felt hats for her dolls and for the bush-tit sock hotels she made for avian tenants.

This was dreamtime with sound: hens, roosters, sheep, wind in the grass, hummingbird wings and rain. She gathered light, framed her projections the way photographers choose their shots, with her fingers, two thumbs and two pointers, a rectangle. Her mother called it Grace TV. "Say Grace," Mum said at the table, and her hippy siblings, Summer and Forrest, made frames, hummed in funky keys and rolled their eyes while Grace got ready to lick her plate and make it laugh, then tell.

"Enjoy. Children are starving in Bangladesh," her mother said, approving of Grace's hunger, spooning out more as she waited for Grace TV.

"What's on today?"

Grace swallowed her mouthfuls and spun her stories, describing a world always moving like clouds across the sky. Sometimes she spun herself, and the colours ran together: rainbow spit, Technicolor smiles. "Fog is tears held in suspension," her mother said, while she sewed muslin bags for the spice she put in her stews and their sheep grew back the wool her father had sheared. "'Cotton' in German is '*Baumwolle*.'" Grace closed her eyes and saw rows of sad-trees shawled in wool.

She's telling me everything means everything, or maybe nothing, Grace thought while she watched birds play hide-and-seek on the infinite screen upstairs, fluffy clouds shaped like her mother's hair, now a lamb, now cantering horses.

She watched mother eagles circle the fields, teaching their young to hunt, to gouge out the eyes of newborn lambs and eat them, what her father called "contemptible snacks."

"Kids need dreamtime," her mother insisted when teachers complained about Grace. Grace TV didn't work on blackboards or lined exercise books, but classroom windows were her silver screens. Grace stared for hours and hours, watched flowers open up in movie time, watched snow make beds where angels lie down and frozen branches blossom.

"Grace is an anomaly, a witness, the essential nonessential invisible in mutable sutras," her fluffy-headed hippy mother explained. The teachers thought Grace's mother should go back to the city she came from and seek help, but Grace thought her mother was special; she understood the beholding.

"You are an uber ewe," Grace said, trying out a new concept, best of the best, snuggling into the soft sweater her mother had spun and knit from clouds of carded wool, combing her mother's tangled wild-woman hair with her fingers, the reason, she said, little girls should not put their fingers in electrical outlets. Grace has not done that. Her hair is straight and auburn like her dad's.

"She's a woolgatherer," her mother apologized to her father when he was annoyed after an eagle stole a newborn lamb from the pasture where Grace had been sent to watch over the flock.

Why did her father call her mother "My Old Lady"?

"He doesn't get us," she told Grace.

That was an aha moment, although Grace didn't realise it until later, when her mother hopped aboard a different cloud and vanished.

Then and now, Grace visits her mother under the willow that weeps like men who can't understand why on Earth their wives would leave them, especially for another woman, where her father buried his AWOL wife's shoes and her purse. What was he thinking, she wonders, that the woman he loved imperfectly would not get far without them?

Ombre, she thinks today, years later, AD, for storm clouds, the black sheep, growers of dark wool and typeface, black on white, ominous script. Now the air smells different. She shifts and closes her eyes. Patterns of light flicker on her lids, herding floaters off the main stage to her mother's things buried under the sorrow tree.

Zap. Zap. Zap. She feels the current, mother to daughter, husband to wife, wife to wife. She understands about electricity, AC/DC, alternating currents. Power shocks. Power failures. Her world is divided in similar ways, everything by halves, Up where her mother wandered into a binary cloud and fell down to Earth, and Down, to After Deaf, nothing to do with religion, miracles, nothing to do with Jesus the time marker, just her way of being, before he turned off the sound.

What happens first, she wonders, do married people

stop listening or does one of them simply turn down the volume?

After her mother drifted away, she grew up, left the farm and found a room in the city, in Chinatown, where she scavenged for images and materials for the small (amuse-bouche?) paintings and collages she sold in street markets and the co-op gallery.

Before Silence, she framed Him with her fingers. She was sketching on the patio at The Ocean Garden, dreaming her way through a pot of Moonlight on the Grove and a plate of fortune cookies when he found her, "Do you mind if I sit here?" Click, her hands went up, made the frame, and her aperture stalled—Northern Chinese, long nose, slender fingers and soft voice. Photogenic.

Magic will transform your life, she read as he pulled up a chair. He talked. She listened. He said he was a magician, and she blinked and read her fortune again.

The human body is an electrical grid, he said, taking her hand, squeezing the little pad between thumb and first finger. She felt a jolt from her groin to her brain, and she couldn't let go because he was pulling her way past the *let go threshold.* Later he observed that he was action, she was reaction, Yin and yang. Perfect. Just like electricity, one electrode jumping to or on another.

He massaged and relaxed her fingers, especially the web parts from the time before, when she was a fish that swam right up to him, sudden love.

Are you hungry, he asked? He whispered in her ear, and he knew what to say, the menu: *shrimp balls, wo wonton, pork buns, green peas with garlic prawns, ginger beef, eight jewel duck with crispy skin, cod with black bean sauce*, in Mandarin and English.

"What do you do?"

"Woolgathering," she said without thinking, when she should have said, "I am an artist." He might have noticed the paint under her fingernails.

"Woolgathering?"

"I dream, and then I translate my dreams into little pictures."

She ate with him. Even before her left brain went along with the decision to stay, she was already there. One mother-generated Grace factoid is that Grace is like a stray cat; once you have fed her, she's yours forever. That was a great family joke.

"Now you've got me," she said, after the magician dipped in the wonton bowl with his soupspoon and slipped a quivery noodle on her tongue.

"The cod's eye is a delicacy," he said when the fish plate arrived. He plucked it out for her, and she saw eagles circling lambs, going for the eyes.

"Then *you* eat it," she said, shivering.

They opened more fortune cookies, and he read his first: *Your dreams will become reality,* and she added words her mother taught her, "in bed."

Later, in his manbed, only a few doors from her studio couch as it happened, he whispered dessert: *lychee nuts, almond cookies, quivering coconut jelly,* and a night-blooming lotus opened between her legs as her private lake trembled then shuddered like fragrant petals reaching for the moon.

So they continued. He practiced his magic tricks, and she moved in, gathered wool and assembled her dreams, cityscapes with clouds, children who looked at clouds and clouds that became animals. Sometimes he surprised her by pulling things from his sleeves, a beautiful scarf or jade earrings. Sometimes he lit flash paper in the dark and startled her out of her sleep.

Every morning rain or shine, she crawled out the bedroom window and sat on the fire escape to watch the sky, and he passed out cups of jasmine tea. Every evening, he whispered in her ear while she held her phone to her other ear, ordering between moans: *ants climbing trees, ma po tofu, moo goo guy pon, bang bang Ji, dragon's beard candy, ginger ice cream.*

By the time the delivery boy came with their cartons, they would be dressed and waiting at the kitchen table—chopsticks, bowls, tea in order and every hair in place. She also moaned when she ate, always licking her plate, making it laugh.

It is the adorable things that first become irritating when the bloom is off the rose.

"Do you have to do that?" he asked, after a while. "You'll lick the pattern off." The pattern was bamboo leaves, very pretty, his mother's china. His mother's flesh was dissolving in a jar filled with wine at the Chinese cemetery. His father's too.

"Earth calling Grace," he complained, when he caught

her gathering, her brush suspended in midair, the paint drying on it. "Earth calling Grace." Sometimes he said it more than once.

"Let's have a child," she said, and he asked if she would pay attention, if her child might drink turpentine or put its fingers in an electrical socket while she was woolgathering.

"You can't just pull babies out of your sleeves," he told her. "You can't put them back when you're having dreamtime."

"You could drop a bomb beside Grace when she's woolgathering," her father advised her lover when he was visiting, meaning, leave her be; *if it ain't broke don't fix it.* But her lover was not used to this sort of proverb. He came from a Confucian family with homilies about social order.

Disorder is not sent down by heaven. It is produced by women.

And fixed by men, of course. It was Chinese New Year, their third together, a time of whispering and feasting. They went to Quon Lee's and bought tins of special New Year's cookies and fireworks wrapped in colourful papers, and even though the bloom was off the rose, they ordered takeout to celebrate in the usual way.

She put on her red silk *cheongsam* and felt how beautifully it fit over the secret child in her slightly swollen belly—so soft, like stroking an animal's flanks. It was the Year of the Horse. She looked out the window and watched white mares canter across the sky. Then she sat down and imagined them galloping through cloud tunnels to the sun. *What is the sound of hooves cantering on air,* she wondered? Her secret child, running in circles around her belly, was still as invisible as air; and she was hungrier than ever.

"Earth calling Grace," he insisted. The delivery boy rang and rang the doorbell.

Her eyes stayed shut. White horses circled the sun, one continuous solar cloud. She heard her lover go downstairs, then up, with paper bags full of sticky rice and singing chicken carolling in his arms.

"Earth calling Grace," he shouted one more time, a warning. He gave warnings when she went off with her dreams. Sometimes he'd bang on their wok with a big metal spoon. This time he went foolish. Stupid. Stupid, especially when they knew a woman who was deaf in one ear because a boy lit a firecracker next to her face.

She heard him strike a match, and then she smelled sulphur.

"Bang!" the room rocked and filled with smoke.

She remembers saying, "Those firecrackers were for New Year's." What a silly reaction when her ears were bleeding, when he might as well have stuck a chopstick in her ear and driven it right through her brain.

They both lost their hearing.

She considered the verb "lost" as if hearing loss was love gone missing, something they might find if they looked hard enough. They looked under the bed, in the phone book, at the clinic. They tried magic, but there were no new ears up his sleeves or inside his top hat, and no enduring love. He was sorry. She was sorry. They took care of one another, although love as they'd known it was forever changed. But it would never be the same.

There would be no more whispering, no more ordering dinner, no more feather dusting the glorious tchotchkes they'd collected in Chinatown and beyond. She found it hard to remember the sound of his voice. Worse, she began to imagine herself ramming chopsticks in his orifices, in his ears, his nose, his anus, driving them right up and into the source of his magic.

He never noticed the child, or if he did, he pretended not to know.

"So long," she said some weeks later, after she'd packed her paints, her brushes, her sketchbooks, her toothbrush and not much else, and left the red silk *cheongsam* on the bed with Proverbs 21, verse 9 pinned to the sleeve.

It is better to live in a corner of the housetop
than in a house shared with a quarrelsome wife.

She moved back to her studio and, shortly after, to the farm. It was too difficult in the city, where crossing the street was dangerous and people asked her if she was deaf or stupid when she read their lips incorrectly, especially the ones attached to their devices. They were the least kind. Who would protect her child from traffic? Who would protect her child from fireworks and people with iPods?

What was the sound of hooves cantering on air? It was still the Year of the Horse. Time to ride home.

The big silver screen still hangs over the field where she's back to her usual, and her father still sings to the rose on her mother's grave; but now it's a silent movie, no murmuration of swallows, no rain on leaves, no bees buzzing or hawks squawking and, most of all, no sheep mother and child radar, familial bleating.

Her father is learning sign language. Grace has been learning to cook lamb short ribs and pineapple upside-down cake, and the rest of her mother's repertoire, root beer chilled in the well and wildflowers in jars. Every afternoon, she lies on her back and watches the sky while the child sleeps inside her.

Once, before he cut the hay, her father almost ran over Grace and her unborn child. Then he jumped right off his tractor, held her and wept under the weeping willow, next to the rose where her mother's purse and her shoes lie buried.

It's past solstice time, time for the sheep to mate and for her baby to arrive. She feels the pull and so does the father of her child, who has sent her a box of divinity with a note. It came in today's mail. *I'm learning to cook, and I've started with divinity candy. Beat egg whites and pour in sugar and the secret ingredient. Nuts are not optional.* She can guess what the secret ingredient might be. She sniffs the candy. It smells familiar. She takes it to the willow tree and eats it, greedily, guiltily because she will not be responding to this overture. It does occur to her to send an egg by return mail. Would it survive? She could wrap it in wool, like an infant. Not.

Solstice or no solstice, it's a firmament-troubled day. She's near her mother, marvelling at how everything changes in a moment: sun to rain, girl to woman, woman to mother. The sky flock is restless. She feels but doesn't hear the thunder and is so intrigued by dark sheep chasing white sheep across the heavens that she fails to run and hide from the lightning that strikes the sorrow tree and invites her child to come suddenly, painfully, jolts of electricity bursting her water right there, no time to get to the house.

Grace is surprised, but calm, alone with her dreaming as usual. Magical thinking will get this life out of her just as it got in. She thinks of her birth canal as a sleeve full of tricks, a silk sleeve filled with fingers and toes stretching and pulling, petals convulsing, opening, flesh-coloured skirts. More lightning. Flash paper. Fireworks, all of it silent. Not a peep from the sky or from her or the willow splitting open, not even the sound of flesh tearing.

The head has crowned. She's crossing the *let go threshold* again, clutched by contrary motion. She pushes, reciting the ingredients for a post-partum menu: savory dumplings, *sik foo,* bitter soup. What was it they ate the day the child was conceived?

More thunder, lightning and rain.

The storm passes. She lies exhausted on her mother's grave with her baby dangling between her legs, its cord still attached, waiting for the next moment to find them. She and her magic trick are soaked with rain and blood, and she shivers, expelling the afterbirth.

Grace and the child doze and wake as the sun slowly warms them. Her *petite jouissance* stretches, brushing her thigh with her fingers. Now she's a mother, her third eye opening. She watches an eagle emerge from its storm shelter at the top of a tall cedar, and she covers the tiny face, remembering the fish eye quivering between her lover's chopsticks.

She doesn't hear the birds. She doesn't hear the ewe approach and paw the ground with her hoof. She doesn't hear the bereft mother rage at the sky that took her lamb. But she does see the eagle vanish, chased away by crows and gulls, raging breath and furious mothers. She undoes the top buttons on her shirt, gathers her slippery child and lifts her to her breast. The baby kneads and gropes with hungry lips and fists, then latches on. Grace is surprised by love. More powerful than lightning or fireworks or lust, the current moves from her nipple to her groin, and she knows it will never let go.

MOUSE, NOT, A SIXTIES SCOOP

This is how I got *out* of jail.

It happened *in* jail. After I joined up with the Brotherhood, we built a sweat lodge and got The Man to let us build a shed for carving. Eventually, we got a bighouse, and that was when my luck changed.

Every year we had two powwows, one in fall and one in spring. At this one powwow, a chief called Running Wolf was the honoured guest. He came in his smudge-face and feathers, and he danced so hard and long for the guys inside, some of the beads fell off his moccasins.

When that happened, all the inmates got down on their hands and knees and looked in the grass for the green beads, but they were impossible to see. He said beads were wisdom, and wisdom was hard to find. The Chief said that was a new four-legged dance called the find-the-bead dance.

Running Wolf wanted to honour someone. All the time, I was thinking how I didn't deserve to be at the powwow and wondering if I had the guts to hang myself or walk into the sea with stones in my pockets. The Chief made a long speech about a brother who gave to others and how he had helped someone in his own family one time. We all wondered who it was—maybe even the warden.

Just then this raven came flying out of the trees and circled the powwow. He landed at the top of a dead cedar.

The Chief held up his fan, and he said it was his most cherished possession. He had it in Vietnam and at Wounded Knee. He said the names of all the warriors who danced with it. Then he called my name, and he gave me his fan, two eagle feathers on an elk antler. He told them I saved one of his nephews who got lost on the street, and I didn't even remember when that happened. I forgot a lot of things when I was drinking, but even when I was most mad at some people, I helped other people.

Getting the eagle feathers was the second gift that changed my life. I've been double blessed. If I ever got lost again, I would let down the Chief and everyone else blessed by that fan. He told me the fan was helping hands and I would fly from then on; and I have.

The first gift came when I took my name back, and that was thanks to a guy who was in jail who had no friends, no one to fan him with sacred feathers like mine.

It's a long story that starts with my real name, Clarence Little Bear Dumont. I got a tall name and a short body, but I wasn't born like that. I was twenty-four inches long the day I got born, and I weighed almost eleven pounds. The doctor at the clinic said that is beyond the normal limit because my mother had gestational diabetes. Lots of Indians have diabetes these days on account of the white man's diet. In my job, I teach people to eat properly, the old way.

My doctor, a nice lady called Maggie who also works with street people, told me I got failure to thrive syndrome. Kids need love and food to grow.

She keeps telling me "bear" is a verb, not just a noun, and people are given the load they can carry. I will know, she says, when it's too much. She thinks I can carry some extra because my heart is big.

I've been sad ever since I can remember, only it's a lot better now. First of all, my dad left when I was three years old. Then my mum drank herself to death. She got drunk one night and went to sleep on her back. Then she choked.

I heard all this from the cousins I met the first time I ran away from the McLeans' house and hitched rides all the way from Victoria to Cortez Island. I was nine years old then.

When I was drinking, I was real careful to sleep on my stomach. That way I wouldn't throw up in my sleep and choke on it like she did.

They said my late mother was born happy. Her Indian name meant "Laughing all the Time." She got real unhappy when my dad left because he caught her in bed with her cousin. That happens, eh. No big deal. She only wanted to stay warm, but my dad didn't like it. The cousins told me he busted the chimney on the wood stove and pushed her down the front steps the day he left. I don't remember all of that time, only the part about me and my brothers and sisters all crying and my mum crying too.

The worst part was the foster home and then the McLeans who adopted me. I don't remember being sad when I lived with my real brothers and sisters. Everyone took care of me then. Even though I was a big baby, they carried me everywhere. My sisters told me that when I met them again.

At the foster home, the white people rubbed my face in my pyjama bottoms when I wet my bed, and they put me in a hot bath and burned me because I wouldn't eat the white people food and cried at night and woke up the other kids.

Indians have got to eat their own food, things like fish and deer meat and wild berries and stuff like that. We get sick when we eat white bread and macaroni. My doctor told me that. And now I'm telling other people. Eat salmon and soap berries and live for a hundred years like our ancestors. She said I was right all along and those foster parents didn't know nothing, except maybe they just didn't care about feeding us right because they were in the foster business to make money from feeding cheap food to Indians.

They had six of us kids in one bedroom. We had to share three to a bed just like at home, but it didn't feel right there because they had a big house with lots of room for more beds. None of us kids got a bicycle or any toys, and we had to do chores all the time. The foster parents sat back and let us do all the work, except the cooking. The foster mother did the cooking. We could have done way better than her.

I got bad scars from those burns the foster parents gave me. I had to go to the hospital, and the social services people went and took back the other kids in the foster home.

The nurses and doctors were nice to me in the hospital. The nurses gave me a teddy bear and all the ice cream I could eat. The hospital smelled bad, and the physio hurt, but at least they treated me nice and said sorry when they put in a needle or made my arms and legs go where they didn't want to.

I met my white stepparents in the hospital. The mother came in dressed like a clown at Christmas and sang songs for all the sick kids. She made animals out of balloons, and you would of thought she was a good person because of that. She kept patting my head and saying "Poor little tyke," and that was real nice.

I like it when people touch me. That didn't happen at the foster home except when the boss hit us with the strap. Sometimes all of us had to lean over our beds with our pants down and get the boss's belt across our bums. He would do that when somebody stole cookies or ate all the lumps in the sugar bowl. Everybody got it because no one would tell who did it. Who would do a thing like that? I still remember the beatings even though I left there when I was five years old.

My new mother found out from the nurses that I needed a home, and she asked if she could take me to her house. She had three kids of her own, and they were all girls. She said she'd like to have a little boy. I heard her say that. I remember it because I couldn't believe my ears. Here was this person who had fun all day long, just like my mum did before my dad left, and she wanted me. I thought if I went to her house, I wouldn't be thinking about my real family all the time, even though I couldn't remember their faces very well anymore.

It was her that read the story about the elephant and the mouse to us kids in the hospital. I thought to myself. I'm gonna be the mouse because everything looks so big to me. The mouse turns out to be the smart one, and I said to myself that's what I'm gonna be. I'm gonna be smart.

What could be smarter than having my new white family coming to the hospital with a new suit for me, and a clean car to ride home in? Before the white parents got me, I thought a lot about my new home. I was gonna live like rich people in the movies: everything shiny and new, lots of clown food in the fridge, no outhouse, and no sharing a bed. I was gonna be a clown prince with all these girls looking after me like before, when my real mother smiled all the time.

The new stepsisters were real shy. The smallest one acted mad when I got to sit in the front seat on the way home. I was up there getting to know my new stepfather.

He squeezed my knee and called me Son. I liked that. My new dad was a lawyer that helped my people, and he was the tallest guy I ever saw. They were all tall, the father, the mother and the new sisters.

It was those girls that started calling me Mouse. At first I liked it, but then it made me real mad, especially when the kids at school found out.

Their house was big and had lots of grass and trees all around it. My job was cutting the grass in the summertime, but I didn't know that for a long time because it was winter when they took me home. I think they should've got a horse to do that job. Then everybody would've been happy—the new family, the horse, the grass and me.

I had my own room. There were cowboys on the curtains and the bedspread, and I should of thought about that. The cowboys had me surrounded, if you know what I mean. I never slept by myself in my life before. The first night I asked one of the new sisters if I could sleep in her bed, and she told on me. The new white mother said they didn't have any of that funny business in their family. I didn't know what she was talking about. I just didn't want to be alone in the dark with cowboys pointing their guns at me.

The first night, we had a big roast of meat with potatoes and vegetables and apple pie with ice cream for supper. Except for the cowboys, things were looking good. I should of known it was all for the guy from the paper who took pictures of everything, the car ride, my room, the first supper, even me standing on a little stool brushing my teeth in my new flannel pyjamas that also had cowboys and Indians on them.

The white mother sure acted different when it was just her and me.

The next day, I had to go to school for the first time. It was hard because those guys already knew each other and I was the only Indian. My stepsisters all had names that started with a J. There was Jane, Jennifer and Justine, who got named after a big boss in Ottawa's kid, even though they didn't know him except for a handshake in a crowd once.

The stepsisters went around telling everyone I was called Mouse and I wasn't a real relation. My people say this prayer when we eat. We hold hands around the table and say, "All my relations." It means everyone in the world is related to everyone else. I wished my new family understood stuff like that.

That first day, I watched my McLean sisters in the lunchroom, and they had lots of food, just like the other kids. They had sandwiches made from the roast we had the night before and apples and bananas and cookies. It was a mystery to me, but I figured it out at suppertime. We got spaghetti with meat sauce, only mine was on a little plate and the girls had big heaps of it. I guess the stepmother saw me looking at their plates, so she explained that I was little kid, and from now on I was gonna get little helpings so I didn't get fat because there was one thing she wasn't going to have in her house and that was a fat Indian.

Look at all those lazy Indians, she said. Did I want to be like them when I grew up? What's wrong with that, I wondered? My mind took a hike into the dining room wallpaper, which was green like a forest. I climbed into a tree and waited for my stepfather to tell her she got it all wrong, but he kept on eating his dinner with his face down. I have to say I got his number right away. He did what she said. She was the boss of that house.

I was putting two and two together and wondering how I was going to grow at all in this kind of a family where the real kids got all the top leaves because they were as tall as giraffes. I guess she never thought that maybe I needed the right kind of food to grow. At the foster home, I hardly ate a thing, just a bit more than my sister. I was so sad. It looked like I was in the same boat all over again. That was the night all my dreams about good times with the rich family went right down the toilet. I wasn't happy there for more than one minute.

None of the kids played with me at recess, but I remember one girl, Lucy, came over to where I was sitting on the swing and gave me her cake because all I got from home for lunch was a carrot and two crackers with cheese in the middle. Anyone with half a brain knows Indians don't like cheese.

Lucy was sad like me because she was a twin and her sister died. "I remember her from before we were born," she said. "Me too," I couldn't believe it. "My sister died at another foster home. She was little like me, and she just stopped eating." Maybe, I thought, Lucy could be my real new sister, more than the McLean sisters, since we were both twins. But it didn't work out that way because Lucy moved to another city right after I met her.

It felt to me like the stepmother went out and got herself an Indian to save herself. I was gonna be her free ticket to heaven. I got homesick right away, but I didn't know what for because I could hardly remember my real family. I just knew they were out there somewhere, and I hoped they were looking for me. At night, I stood beside the cowboys in my curtains and looked out my bedroom window and wondered if my brothers and sisters were looking at the sky too, trying to figure out which star would bring them to me, like baby Jesus.

I chose myself the big one that still shines in the morning. My stepfather told me that one was called Venus. He knew all about the stars and stuff like that. The best part of living with the new family was finding out what my stepfather learned from the books he read at night after supper.

Every time I ran away from home, I followed that Venus star, and it took me to some interesting places, like the river where I made a fort and cooked fish on the beach until the day the fishing police busted me. Another time it took me to the back door of a bakery where there were all these pies waiting for someone to eat them. I ate blackberry pie until I was sick in a bush. That sure tasted better than the food the stepmother gave me to eat. Once it took me to a place down some stairs where men were dancing with men, and this guy dressed like a woman took me home and looked after me real good until the cops came to take me back.

The stepmother wanted me to be white, and I had a problem with that. In the foster home, the parents were mean, but at least the other kids were Indians too. They were more like real brothers and sisters. We got to laugh at stuff after lights out, and we helped each other with problems. None of the stepsisters were going to help me with their mother, because they were too busy staying out of trouble themselves. They snitched on me when I stole food from the kitchen, and they didn't let me touch their toys and books. It was like I'd get them dirty.

The stepmother was always going on about Indians. If my shirt didn't match my pants, she'd say, "Mouse, we don't dress like Indians in this house." One time when she dropped me off at a white kid's birthday party, I heard her tell the mother to make sure I didn't steal nothing. I could feel that mother's eyes on me the whole time, and my stomach hurt so much I couldn't enjoy the cake.

One time I got this valentine from that library lady we had. She said I was her special friend, and that didn't sound at all bad to me. The stepmother made me carry the same lunch kit to school every year, and I was there for a total of seven or so years. Some kids teased me because of my little lunches, and they kicked my box around.

By grade six, my lunch kit was a real mess. The cowboys were dented in so bad it looked like they'd all been kicked in the ass by a buffalo, and the top was coming off its hinges. I begged the stepmother, but she said, no way. I even thought about not taking a lunch at all, but I was too hungry all the time for that.

The library lady must've figured this out. She saw how sad I was at lunchtime, I guess. When I came to school on Valentine's Day, there was a shiny new lunch kit on my desk. It didn't have cowboys on it. It had Charlie Brown and Lucy. When I opened my new lunch kit, I saw it was full up with valentine cards and candies. The library lady didn't say it was her that left it for me, but I saw her looking at me with this big grin on her face, so I knew. It was Mrs. James.

That was one of the best days of my life. I was so happy I had wings on my feet. I was so stoked, but that didn't last long. The stepmother took it away from me and brought it right back to the school. She took me with her, and she made me sit on the steps while she shouted so loud at the principal I heard every word.

She said I had to learn how to take care of things. Indians didn't know how to do that. They had to be taught. She said the library lady did a bad thing. The principal got mad right back, but the stepmother didn't listen. She made me leave it all: the leftover candies—the cards—every last thing.

I was glad I ate all the jelly heart things on the bus before I got home.

My school days were hard; especially when we left Moss Rocks and went to Central and then Vic High. No one was ever mean to me, not like they were to that kid Evelyn that got himself beat up for wearing a dress, but I didn't have real friends. Sometimes I wished Lucy would come back, but she didn't. I seen kids looking at me like I was different, and I guess I was. When the guys started to grow in junior high, I never. It made me feel real bad. The stepmother kept rubbing it in too.

One time I was teaching myself how to fix stuff. I had an old typewriter and a radio I got at a yard sale with a pile of free stuff, and I took them apart in my room. I knew where all the pieces went, only she didn't believe me. She said my room looked like a nuisance ground. Then she loaded me in the car and took me for a long drive. In the beginning, I liked it because we stopped at a drive-in and had a hamburger for lunch, and then we drove up the Malahat. It's real steep, and until I got to the lookout, all I saw was rocks and trees. From the top, I could see the whole world, the ocean, the land, the sky, lots of birds and boats in the water. I never seen anything like it before.

That stepmother talked nice until we got to Cowichan Bay. I hoped she was turning over a new leaf, but that was too good to be true. Cowichan Bay felt real familiar, the ocean and the hill with the stone church on it. I wanted to jump out of the car as soon as I seen it. We drove past the Indian cemetery, and some graves had toys on them for little kids that went to heaven and some had plastic flowers, so I wondered which one might be my late mother and my sister.

Thinking about her gave me this sad feeling in my stomach. I looked over at the stepmother driving the car with her mean mouth, and I thought she was as ugly as a woman can get. It's funny because when I saw her at the hospital in her clown clothes, I thought she was nice-looking. It doesn't take much for a woman to make herself ugly.

She starts pointing at people's houses and asking me if I wanted to live in a dump like that. She and my new family were giving me a chance to be a chief. Did I want to be an Indian with cars all over the yard? I wanted to ask her what was the point of growing grass and flowers we can't eat instead of having spare parts for your car, but I could tell she wasn't gonna listen anyway, so I just let her talk.

The truth was, I *did* want to be an Indian. That was the day I really decided. I'd rather be an Indian with cars in his yard than a woman with a big house where nobody laughed.

I didn't say one word all the way home, and I guess she thought I was thinking about how I could be a good boy and remember to clean my room and wear socks that matched. Actually, I was thinking how easy it would be to steal her car and get back to Cowichan Bay and wondering who would hide me from her when I got there. I had a hunch I had relatives on that rez, and I was right.

The first time I took the Volvo for a spin, I got caught by the cops, and they made me wait right there on the street 'til the stepparents showed up mad as hell. It was three o'clock in the morning. "Do you know what time it is, Mouse," my stepfather kind of growled at me. Of course I did. I wasn't so stupid I'd steal a car in broad daylight. I waited until everyone in the house was asleep, then I took the stepmother's keys from the hook by the door and rolled the car down the driveway. It was dead easy. I must have driven around for about an hour, honking at chicks and enjoying all the bright lights.

Driving her car was no problem. I'd been taking it in and out of the driveway every time they went out since I was about thirteen years old. The only hard part was reaching the pedals. I guess the cops saw a short guy behind the wheel and wondered. I got busted before I even crossed Cook Street.

The stepmother was threatening to send me to a shrink for a long time because I wasn't fitting in. It is hard to fit into a family of tall people when you are short and everyone makes you feel small all the time. The car thing finally tore it, she said. I was acting like an Indian in spite of all her sacrifices. I told her Indians don't steal cars from white people, they just borrowed them, but she didn't get it. She made me get in the car, and she drove me over to that guy Catchpole's house, and I had to answer a lot of questions that were none of his business.

Dr. Catchpole is the guy I met up with in William Head Prison. I was in for lighting fires, and he was there for what he did to kids like me. Someone finally told. You better believe there was nobody there to bless him with feathers.

The first thing I didn't like about Dr. Catchpole was the way he looked at himself in the mirror he had across from his desk when he was supposed to be talking to me. Not that I said anything much. It made me mad to think he wasn't listening anyway. I wasn't going to ever say a word to someone who was so much in love with himself he couldn't hear the people that paid him money to hear their stories. It wasn't my money. It was the government's, but that's not the point. The point is, he wasn't doing his job right.

"I'm gonna burn down your house," I mumbled one afternoon when it was so hot I couldn't get my mind off the discount popsicle I was gonna grab on the way home. I had to do business that way because my stepparents never let me have money.

"What?" he said.

"Is the furnace on in your house?" I asked. "It's real hot in here." Catchpole said he wanted me to be in his club. He'd got all these kids he was supposed to be helping to do work. There were lots of chores to do. Some kids did the weeding and stuff like that. The special ones got to work in the greenhouse where he grew his orchids. I never went in there, and it was a good thing because bad stuff happened to the orchid boys. I heard about it from Tommy. I think he said the orchid boys had to eat dirt.

I've been eating dirt and bologna all my life, so I was real careful. I wasn't going to be anybody's slave, especially after the foster home where even babies had to work. I was nice to Dr. Catchpole because of the sports games, and movies and pizzas. I figured if I went along with it, I could have some fun. I wasn't in it for the uniform like some of the kids. They liked dressing the same, but I didn't. That didn't feel right to me. It wouldn't help me get any closer to being an Indian, which was all I ever wanted.

One day Dr. Catchpole asked me if I wanted to come over for a barbeque, and I did. I thought about steak frying on the pit all the way over there on the bus, and I thought about roasting marshmallows with the boys, which we did at the last barbeque. We called the black layers of burnt sugar "underwears" and pretended we were taking off girls' panties. Then we licked our fingers, and they tasted sweet and burnt. Mmhmmm. We talked about girls when Dr. Catchpole wasn't listening. He didn't like us to talk dirty, just like the other grown-ups. Dr. Catchpole liked being one of the boys, but when it got right down to it, he was just another cop.

When I got to his place that day, there were no other boys there. Not one. Just me. He had the barby all fired up, and I could see two beautiful steaks sitting on a big plate. They were thick as my foot, and they covered the whole platter. Boy, you should of heard my stomach growling. All I ever got for breakfast at my new parents' house was a bowl of yoghurt and a glass of orange juice. Who ever heard of Indians eating yoghurt?

I said yes to the steak, and Dr. Catchpole wrapped some spuds in tinfoil, and we filled them up with bacon and stuff when they were cooked. After we ate the steak and potatoes and some cut up tomatoes, he asked me if I wanted to see his orchids.

I should of known there was a catch. He grabbed my hand and wouldn't let go. His garden turned red on me. The trees and the flowers were on fire and big petals reached out to swallow me. Even Dr. Catchpole's eyes turned red, and he looked like the devil. I seen kids come out of that greenhouse. I watched them turn from happy boys into jumpy bone racks. I had to get out of there, but I knew if I ran, Dr. Catchpole would catch me. I was worried he would tie me up in there and let the ants eat me, and that gave me an idea.

Dr. Catchpole and me used to talk a lot about that guy called Harry Houdini who got himself out of ropes and chains. I told him I was feeling like that, and I didn't know how to get myself out of that white family and be an Indian. He said I could if I wanted to. It wasn't hard if you really wanted to. He said he would show me. I could tie him up with ropes, and he would show me how to get free. Even though the garden was on fire and everything was hot to touch, I said I was ready. First, I would tie him up, and he would show me how to free myself. Then he would tie me up. Then we could go to see the orchids, because I wouldn't be afraid anymore.

He liked that idea. He said going to the greenhouse was my reward. I tried to stop my hands from shaking. He said it was a breakthrough and I should be real excited. Times like that made him glad to be a shrink, because money wasn't enough for his kind of work. He sent me to get the rope from the garage where he kept his big van and his sports car. That gave me another idea. I picked up his rope and went back to the garden. Dr. Catchpole was sitting on this garden chair, and he says, "Tie me up, Mouse."

I already told him not to call me Mouse.

I got Dr. Catchpole to hold one end of the rope, and I started circling it round and round him. I kept the rope real tight, just like doing up your shoelaces. I could see he thought he was smarter than me because he was breathing in lots of air and making his muscles big. He was smiling, and I could hear him thinking he was going to bust out in no time flat. Then I would see how easy it was to get out of jail and he would take me to the orchids.

All the time I was making the rope as tight as I could, I was thinking Mouse, Mouse, and I remembered going to the reserve with the stepmother and hearing the rude things she said about my people. I thought about her correcting me all the time and trying to get me to talk like her people and the little lunches I got at school and the time I got put in the hot bathtub. I saw red. I was a see-red hopping-mad Indian.

What Dr. Catchpole didn't know was I was real good at tying knots. My stepfather taught me that stuff. He wasn't all that bad, not like his wife. Every time I twisted that rope around my shrink, I tied the biggest knot you ever saw. My stepfather said even God couldn't undo a knot like the ones I made. Dr. Catchpole sure tried. It was great watching his face lose that shit-eating grin when he was thinking about getting out and taking me to the greenhouse where those orchids were gonna eat me alive. He tried and he tried, just like the big bad wolf, but he couldn't do it."

"Mouse," he said. "You win. Untie me now." I could hear in his voice that he was scared of me, and it made my heart sing.

"My name is Clarence," I said. "Clarence Little Bear Dumont, and I am strong."

"Enough's enough, Clarence," he tried to sound like a cop, but I could tell he was scared. "Not on your life," I said, jingling the keys that I took out of his pocket, and I thought about going back to the garage and getting some gas and setting him on fire, but I didn't.

I was lucky I didn't go to jail that time because I got my first taste of the joint a little later on and I didn't like it one bit. I would've spent my whole life in there if I did that. While I was wondering what to do next, I thought about what was gonna happen to me, if I was going to have a sad ending or a happy ending. The whole idea was to have a happy ending. That's the kind of story I like. I like it when the mouse is smarter than the elephant and everything works out OK.

So I just left him there. It was good enough for me that I could imagine the fire burning all around him even if he couldn't. I don't know how long he had to wait. I hope he peed himself. Maybe one of the boys came and untied him after a while. I kind of hope he was on the ground so that boy got to feel tall the way I was feeling when I drove that red sports car up the Malahat yelling "Goodbye Mouse. Hello Clarence Little Bear Dumont" at the top of my lungs.

That was the day I got my name back. It still took a while to get to where I am today. I had to start a few real fires and go to the slammer, but soon I ran into Chief Running Wolf and learned from him that helping people was going to be my job, and not just something that happened a few times. Now, thanks to real nice people like him, I have a social work degree, and there are gardens in all the parks where my street friends can grow their own food.

K'o'yetsin, I'm a bear that fights for my people. Stronger together. I'm grateful to everyone that done me a favour, because they helped me grab my power, even Dr. Catchpole, who's out of jail now and working at the needle exchange. Sometimes I buy him a coffee. Someone bad did it to him too. I got to remember that.

LIPSTICK WINDOW

We live on number 11, near the Chemainus River, and every fall when the cottonwood leaves change colour, the *Zhum* swim up for spawning. There's lots of costume changes going on in that river. The ladies start out in silver dresses that blink like phosphorus on the Salish Sea. My girlfriend says, don't look, they're changing underwater, and by the time they get to the logjam, they're all wearing red.

That tells the guys they are ready to make holes in the gravel and lay their eggs, gives the signal to cover them up.

By then, the men are looking ready, with hooked noses and bars that mean they're going for the forever stretch. I don't tell my girlfriend that because she wants to get married, and I'm not telling her I already know marriage is just a joint with benefits. I think this hunger she's got is why she's been wearing that dress I like. I know she leaves lipstick kisses on the bathroom mirror when she goes out to knit with her friends so I won't forget her.

"I'll be back. I always come back."

I call it the lipstick window because I can see the future in it, maybe not what I'd choose if I had my way.

But she's got my back. Once she traded a sweater for my Ray-Bans. There isn't one thing that goes by without me seeing it, not the big smilie who thinks he's smarter than me, or the tiniest stonefly nymphs. If the fish could talk, they'd say, Weez has X-ray vision.

There's a lot of battles in the river too. I've never seen a *Zhum* wearing Ray-Bans, but they watch their backs. When they go at it, the river splashes something fierce. I watch all this and pick my fight, just one every year, one dog that is bigger and meaner than the rest. I watch and wait, and at the end of the day, he takes the hook and does his time in my smoker.

This magic business happened the year my sister and her baby went to spirit, when I'm chasing after the one called Boss. He was the best; and in the end, I had to let him go, even though I been after him for days and days.

One night Boss is playing with me, swimming right up and giving me stink eye, then disappearing inside that twist of branches that fell in the river after the big storm last year. He does it so many times it takes all I have to stay still and ignore him. One of us has to wear out first, and it isn't going to be me. I sit down and almost fall asleep against that big cedar tree with roots that go straight to the river, the best ones for making baskets.

Crow wakes me up with her storytelling. I always listen to her. She makes more sense than most people. When she takes off, I see her fly around the moon.

The moon is full, and all the lights are on in the forest beside the river. I hear a sound like wooden bracelets, and then I see a sliver of light between the trees. Since I smoked a joint earlier, I think my eyes are playing tricks on me. The next day, I can't stop thinking about it, wondering if it could be the wolf that stalked my sister and stole her baby, or maybe my sister's ghost. She did a stupid thing after her baby went to sleep in the river. She put a .22 right in the middle of her forehead. I've got to go after my daughter, she told me before she did it. Nothing I could do.

The next night, it happens again, and the next. I start sleeping all day so I can stay awake at night. I don't want to miss her. I know it's her. I've always been waiting for something and right away I know it's all been practice for getting my sister back. She'll have a lot to tell us about the other side camp. Maybe she'll bring her daughter with her.

The ghost smells like cedar boughs after the rain. I keep hearing those wooden bracelets and the swish of her skirts.

I know it isn't the white woman who has her eye on me. She breaks twigs.

I make a mistake and tell my girlfriend about it. She gets mad and tells me I'm supposed to be thinking about her all the time and not about a dead woman or a woman who watches me fish. Then she goes to stay with her own sister and leaves me to finish the business with mine. No problem. I don't want to keep on sharing this story with her. I know what I know, and I don't want to have to explain it to anybody.

Boss leaves too. He finds his mate, goes for his logjam honeymoon, and then he dies. I feel a shiver up my back. It's like someone else in my family went to spirit.

The leaves fall from the tree, and it's my birthday time. That's what my name means, *Xwixelanexw.*

I stay away from the sweat lodge all winter because I don't want to run into the crazy river and step on him. I like to swim with fish, but I don't much like the idea of fish spirits oozing between my toes, especially his.

It takes such a long time for this winter to be over. I catch lots more fish and smoke them, and every night I go back to the river and wait. My sister was a night person. All night long, she told stories and laughed so hard she shook our bed. I look up at the sky and hear her.

My sister's star is a far walk, a galaxy away from mine. But, like I said, I'm a patient man, and *Zhum* has the longest journey.

My girlfriend comes back and says she's sorry and it's high time she had a ring on her finger, so I take some advice from the guy at the gas station, and I go online and order her a ring for fifty bucks. She gets a piece of paper saying that star has her name on it, but she still wants more, even a real diamond. That's a joke and a half.

Did I say my sister's name is Starlene?

Starlene keeps slipping through the trees, laughing

at me, like we used to play hide-and-seek in the forest. Usually I found her because she was noisy. I even hide in the river because I can hold my breath and stay underwater for a long time.

This one yellow cedar has a strip of bark missing. It could be rabbit or a deer, or it could be one of the elders making canoe balers. In any case, I keep my eye on her. When the spring rain is done, I peel more bark. It's like taking off Star's dress, the one with her blood all over it after she put the bullet in her head. It comes off real easy, and I work fast because I don't like to be reminded.

I taste the wood, and it is sweet. Crow makes a sound like water.

On the night of the full moon, I fall asleep on the ground, and I dream I'm carving. The rest of her dress falls away, and the yellow cedar cuts easy as butter. It sings under my knife, the sound of waves and wind in the cedar boughs. I let it go where it wants. It carves a moon face rising from her shoulders, hummingbirds sipping her milk and Eagle giving her a ride to the other side camp.

The tree shivers. That wakes me up. There's wind this night, and the branches shake and moan, and the silver ghost rises out of the tree and up to a glass door in the moon. She goes in backwards, looks back and raises her hands to me.

When the glass door shuts, she leans into it and kisses it. I see her lipstick in the moonlight. It is bright red. She leaves a lot of kisses. I see her woman shape in the sky.

I leave the river and go home to my girlfriend. I won't return until the salmon come back.

My girlfriend says she's having a baby and we have to get married right away. I say OK. Maybe it will be a girl. We'll call her Starlene.

UTMOST HAPPINESS

They're real," I say.

"How do you know?"

"I just do."

"That's a lame argument from a philosopher."

"Caroline, you tell me, did I go through twenty-three hours of labour for this?"

"This what?"

"Disrespect."

"Call it what you like. You chose it. You always get to choose."

"Call it what you like," indeed: djinns, fairies, genies, bad actors paid to make me crazy, or hallucinations, I am not on drugs, and I do see them. Soundless, except maybe the whirring of wings, a pitch that is not normally in my spectrum and could be my imagination; the human-sized creatures turn up at dusk and at dawn, and they seem desperate to tell me something, those frantic damselflies, dragonflies, injured feelings and mutating crows.

"I should never tell you anything. You always overheat."

My daughter says she thinks she might have planted the seed long ago, and I'm retro-channeling the hermit or whoever lived in the woods behind her elementary school. When she tentatively mentioned him, as if maybe she shouldn't have, I worried he might be a pervert, some sanctioned, possibly blessed elderly pedophile gently nudged from active duty, a former teacher or priest from some faraway parish. For sure, he never showed himself when we dropped off and picked up our kid.

The schoolbus driver, a Cowichan elder well-acquainted with spirits and spirit dancing, knew about him, but he just shrugged his shoulders. "Nothing to report," he said. The same thing the Catholic School Board said about the long-time driver and cultural teacher when a student turned him in for inappropriate touching, which may or may not have happened. He used to pat the kids on the bum before they got off the bus and say their names. "Goodbye Charlie. Goodbye Angela. Goodbye Xwixelanexw." He knew all their names. I was impressed.

When it rained in those days, I wondered if the woods and the streets would flood with laterally assigned clergy, blessing the kids with their equivalent of holy water.

The priest came to visit. He sat in the rocking chair beside our woodstove and gulped the sipping whiskey we'd been saving for something special. And this was special. We hoped it would loosen his lips. But it didn't.

Didn't the school give shelter to motherless kids from the rez? Didn't the church give the Boat People free tuition? What's the problem with a hermit minding his own business, contemplating God's grandeur in the woods?

I was an expert on perverts who lived in forest shacks. For one, the witch who lured Hansel and Gretel to her candy cottage and fattened them up for the kill. For two, The Ranger who patrolled the forest around the golf-course where I grew up, and on the pretence of looking for lost golf balls, kidnapped and boiled little children alive. For three, all the Highlanders who danced out of the woods where I'd walked to school with their kilts tilting in the wind, offering up the whole menu from appetizer to dessert, a taste of amuse-bouche to the whole banana. Flambé.

So I took it to the Headmistress.

"Are you kidding," I did not ask but said to the Top Sister, her powdery paper-thin skin blanched in the Lamb of God's formadehyde footbath. I had noticed that all the sexless ones were pasty pale. The wankers who confessed to lesbian and or Jesus fantasies had rosy cheeks. That's how you told them apart. The rosy-cheeked nuns were more compliant to anarchy and more likely to excel at baseball.

According to my mini-snitch, the Hermit lived in a Hogan, a circular half-underground structure with sod walls. She was too scared to check inside, but she embellished her story with details I realized she'd picked up from visits to the museum.

The Hogan was surrounded by gardens neatly contained in stone perimeters and joined by paths guarded by sword ferns and huckleberry bushes. In short, it was a fairyland, and from time to time, fantastic creatures appeared in Forest tableaux.

No one seemed to know what the Hermit looked like, whether he was a pasty clergyman or a hobo in rags, but there were many reports about the half-human creatures, some covered in leafy camouflage and some feathered, giant ravens and woodpeckers, northern flickers who appeared, frozen, between the trees, and seemed to stun the witnesses who saw but could not pursue them.

"They just turn up and stare at us, and we freeze. By the time we think to reach out and touch them, they, poof, disappear, like a bubble popping."

It was about that time that I witnessed a miracle, an erythronium opening in a forest clearing, one lily-white petal at a time. Was I living in a zone where transformation was the norm, where spirits entered and left the bodies of aboriginal dancers, and crows imitated every sound in nature, a barking dog one minute and wind in the leaves the next? Or was I just a hysteric looking for signs that lead to redemption of revelation or whatever rehabilitation my soul needed, because God knows, I have sinned.

Maybe it has to do with giving up religion, not once but several times, the first being when I tossed my virginity in retaliation for parental abandonment and the last when a priest with a gorgeous singing voice (and yes, I did know about Sirens) let loose a spew of bigotry about the Japanese, some of whom had, in fact, built the very pulpit from whence he was ranting. I walked out on his sermon and a choir I loved singing in and never came back.

It was shortly after that when my daughter reported on the hermit, and I started seeing fantastic woodland creatures. But that was thirty-plus years ago, and I thought I was done with it.

"Could be genetic memory, Ma," my daughter says. She's a horticulturist and knows all the great names and big garden styles, from Abdalonymus to Vita Sackville-West, whose white garden at Knowles we visited the year Caroline graduated from high school.

"In Europe, before they colonized Canada, our wealthier ancestors hired mimes to pose in their gardens, and the poorer ones watched commedia dell' arte and Punch and Judy in the streets."

"What does *that* have to do with *this*?" I am shaking my gin, not Djinn, at the end of a long day of screen-staring and talking to her on the phone. She has a calming voice, a peri-menopausal mezzo, unlike my own mouse-whine, which, although good for treble singing, is unpleasant to live with. I hate listening to myself.

"Too much typing, not enough digging. You're letting the weeds take over."

"It's true, the anarchists are winning." That is a valid comment on my brain *and* my overgrown garden that, without my glasses, is English wild, more Capability Brown than *House and Garden*, but, in truth, has given way to morning glory and blackberry brambles.

"My garden is me," I say. "I'm a little overgrown

too. We match."

"Yes, but you've always said how working with your hands relaxes you."

"I am working with my hands." I type a few words so she can hear me.

"Not the same."

"Don't want to disturb the little families." At the moment, we have robins nesting in an apple tree, a hummingbird hotel in a japonica, bush-tit socks in a pine and an amazing wasp condominium in the compost.

"Excuses," she says.

"I hate over-trained gardens. *That* is genetic."

My grandmother created a park in a Garry oak meadow by the sea, plantings in wild brushstrokes, even the vegetable garden. The best part was the fairy glen where I played with invisible friends all summer long.

"Me too."

"Your canon," I said.

We come from a family of writers. She writes with colour and texture, every word growing out of the soil.

"I am astonished by how many great writers were also notable gardeners."

"And a lot of them were in looney bins."

"Which also had great gardens."

"Only for the rich. Bedlam was not so sweet."

"You're always practical."

"Maybe getting practical would get your head out of your ass, Ma. You've been obsessing, about politics for one."

"Pretty unavoidable, given the state of the world."

"All the more reason to change gears."

"No more panto in the rhododendrons."

When she was little, we played charades on special occasions. We guessed book and movie titles and, when there were presents involved, "guess the gift." She couldn't nail her birthday tutu covered in leaves and rosebuds, so I kept it for six months past her magical garden party and offered it again on Christmas, by which time it was too small.

"I'm sorry about the tutu."

"I wasn't that into ballet, Ma. That was your thing. I was more than happy with my pint-sized gardening tools."

"If I'm not atoning for …that, it… has to be something else."

"You'll think of it."

"I always do."

"Yes." She hung up.

I was too embarrassed to go back to the store after I shoplifted a lipstick. I'd been distracted by a woman with no money who was leaving without her groceries, and when I chased her out of the store to offer to pay, I accidentally dropped the lipstick in my pocket. I could have returned and paid for it. I was too much in love and too young to think that my lover had a wife and children. I was too intimidated to call my mother-in-law a racist. I sometimes buy vegetables in plastic packaging. I flushed the toilet in Cuba when there were water restrictions. I spanked my daughter. I eat therapeutic cheese puffs, all brands, orange fingers a giveaway. I have lied to vegetarians about my soup. There is almost always chicken in my stock. I try to recover spiders from the bathtub and put them out the window, but sometimes I squeeze them to death.

The list is endless. Are the garden creatures here to forgive me or remind me?

"Don't let it in the house," my husband says when I tell him about spotting a crow with a six-foot wingspan hovering over the gate when he comes home for dinner.

"But they never speak."

"When did that ever stop you?"

The phone rings. My daughter interrupts us. This has always been her calling.

"Don't you have potatoes to hill?"

"Sorry, Ma, but you've got me worried. Have you been outside, extended your eyes, relaxed your mind?"

"Sure, and I saw a giant crow."

"Snap it and put it on Facebook."

"You mean, alongside the walrus doing sit-ups."

"That's right."

"Would you comment and call it alternate news?"

"Maybe."

"So the camera lies too?"

"Everything lies."

I have raised a cynic. Congratulations to me.

"Something else to put on my list."

"What?"

"Nothing." I don't have to explain everything. If you

don't get it right away, you'll have to wait for Christmas. That's my rule. I am not into plot exegesis.

I'm reading Arundhati Roy's new book, *The Ministry of Utmost Happiness*, the story of a two-spirit hijra. Some small part of me wants to know if she has found *it*, if transformation is the key. I know my best captures have been in-between the expected and the unexpected, moments of magical thinking, the time I jumped off a cliff and the wind carried me up, then let me down gently, and when I surprised myself by riding an updraught and expelling an egg in an explosion of rain.

Soon rain will cycle back again. So far in this season of alternating moods, there has been no need to irrigate the trees and the lawn. The garden is still. From the roof, where I am sitting with my binoculars and a martini with three olives, my world looks as it always has: no pine beetles, no smog and no gnawing hunger. Everything is fed, the grass and the trees have water, the birds drink from their fountains, and the humans can safely eat vegetables with the dirt still on them. The clematis is blooming. Glorious peonies hold their sleepy heads up. Hummingbirds are feeding, and baby robins express gratitude that their mother is home with food in her beak.

But we do live in an earthquake zone. We are ready and not ready for this. We have provisions, medicine, food and a tent, stored in a safe place. That is ready. Beyond ready, there are the surprises. Not ready includes Earth opening and swallowing people we love, injuries we cannot tend, grief we cannot assuage, especially if we survive those more deserving, closer to their productivity, our daughter for example, a healer who creates beauty and grows medicinal plants. She is needed.

I call her back. "Are you OK?"

"Why wouldn't I be?" she asks. "I am not the crazy one."

"Crazy like a fox," I say. "Did you know the Conservatives in Britain are trying to reinstate fox hunting."

"It never ended."

"The Manichean heresay," I say.

"Yes. Are you taking your sleep meds?"

"Sometimes." That is the truth. I have saved a bunch, just in case the pain is too great or her father dies first, or the Conservatives are re-elected here.

She is intuitive. "By the way, you aren't really going to give Dad that Deadguy T-shirt for his birthday are you? Tell me you made that up."

"I make everything up, recipes, theorems, poems..."

"NO seriously, Ma, that might hurt his feelings."

"It would hurt my feelings if he died before me."

"It would rain tears."

"What language does the rain speak?"

"Oh Ma, now you've put a flea in my ear."

"Not me, a better poet."

"I won't forget it."

"Good."

I already told her I have a plan to keep him warm if he insults me by refusing to wake up one morning. That involves pipes and hot water, turning him into a human radiator. She asked me why, and I told her I needed someone for giggles and cuddles. When she protested that dead men don't joke, I told her just thinking about it made me laugh. She didn't get it, but why would she, the young never think about dying.

I hear conversation and look down.

"Wait. There is someone in the garden. Three someones. Hang on in case it's a home invasion."

"I'll call the cops. It might be something." She's playing me. Something, it turns out, two men, one woman and a lost drone.

"Whaaat?"

"It's true. Her friends gave it to her for her birthday, and they're teaching her how to use it."

She has one leg up the apple tree, but I have to stop her.

"Sorry, no shaking. There are baby robins living there."

"Sorry." They answer in unison.

"They are speaking, Caroline. They are real in your terms."

"This is more than I can absorb," my daughter says.

We hang up. At the same time.

The drone searchers tenderly move the branches until their strange little creature falls out. They thank me and leave. I take a photo. I did not imagine them.

We have a salad on the verandah, and night eventually falls, as it usually does. My husband decides it's his bedtime. I am the night owl who tucks things in: children, pets, the house. When I cover the canary, turn off the lights and go out to the verandah to admire the moonlight, I notice an owl sitting on top of a broken cedar in the park, where the eagles nest. Like the crow I saw earlier this evening, it is giant. I do hear its wings beat, then glide, consonants and vowels as it lifts off from the evergreen tree and heads straight toward me. Closer, I see a human head; it could be a seraph, its song is ferocious. I think I see fire coming out of its beak.

"*Sinestra, Sinestra*," it says, then disappears in an explosion of stars and feathers that float to the ground like snow. Time to go in.

Using celestial navigation, I take my medicine with another shot of gin. Who's counting?

My husband is waiting in bed, reading. I decide not to to mention my owl. He takes off his glasses and puts down his book, the biography of a dead friend, the one who wrote, "How can I miss you if you won't go away?" and turns out his night light. I visualize him in the T-shirt that is wrapped and hidden with his other gifts in the closet.

"What's so funny?" he asks.

"Life," I say.

"We've had a good run, lots of music, lots of stories, good friends and bad."

"Caroline, who is both."

"She loves you, Cynthia."

"Yes." I kiss his shoulders.

"Good night," he says.

"Goodbye," I say.

MOON CAKE AND RUDE HOUR

When she boils the eggs for her moon cakes, he reminds her to prick the ends for easy peeling. "Do I look like an idiot?" How many times has he checked the stove to see if she remembered to turn it off? How many times has he asked if she remembered her glasses, or put her credit card back in her wallet?

Who is the real prick here?

When she closes her eyes, he looks like an egg. She imagines him rolling off the end of the world, "Adios, Babycakes. *Hasta luego*. Not."

No one gets between her and her impulses, her enthusiasms. Not even him.

She reads the haiku on the two-by-two-inch piece of rice paper she planned to fold into the dough, then puts it in her mouth, chews and swallows. Perhaps he will see it in the toilet later. To conserve water, they only flush when necessary. She wonders if he will be curious enough to fish it out.

Man Squirrel hides nuts
she finds and bakes
in slices of harvest moon.

He wonders about her pet sentiments; squirrels are just rats with bushy tails, he says, but he does admire their resourcefulness as nut and candy robbers, their frantic autumnal activity. “It’s cute, but shut the windows anyway. You don’t want them nesting in the house and inviting their city cousins.”

Trees on fire, this is her favourite time of year. She is an avid non-religionist, celebrates all the fall festivals—*Eid, Diwali, Sukkot,* Halloween, *Dia de los Muertos,* Thanksgiving—especially the food parts: apple pie, pumpkin pie, sugar skulls and moon cakes. She’s prepared, has moulds and doodads for everything. Her moon cake mould is a chrysanthemum, the most resilient of the four gentlemen flowers of the Chinese seasons. It’s made of rubber, possibly toxic. She imagines her cake blowing up in the oven, exploding like the trees in the park where she sits for hours and hours and watches the autumn leaves flaring, crumpling and tumbling, sleeping in piles.

So far, nothing uber-dramatic has happened, apart from the forever surprise, a perfect cake every time. Her happy hens cooperate, hold off on their strikes until after her frenzy of fall baking: sponge for *Sukkot,* moon cakes, Thanksgiving pumpkin pies. She rewards her girls with fresh greens, squashes and cabbages, chicken footballs, and they keep on laying for her, sumptuous autumn yolks—bright, bright yellow, rich as harvest moons.

She loves the warm cosiness of feathery chicken breasts, going to the henhouse in the garden and gathering a comfort of eggs in her straw-filled basket; sees herself as a hen laying fragile ideas with nurturing yolks. Her ferocity is maternal, she thinks. She is drawn to the egg shape, to the master Brancusi, whose hatched sculpture was disappointing. *Garder les oeufs* is her motto. Eggs R Us.

This time, for spite, for the anarchist ladies, she does not prick the ends, but brings the water slowly to a boil, then turns off the heat, wondering if it is better to die like this, in increments, the way the Earth itself is heating up so the oligarchs can deny it is happening. She puts in her left hand and leaves it until she can't take the heat.

While her mother grooved in the gay corridors of privilege in the American Empire: The Factory, Studio 54, Le Pavillon, their Bible-thumping nanny lectured her about the right hand of God, tied her left hand behind her back and made her eat with her right. When she spilled, she was punished. "Look what the devil made you do!"

Now she will make moon cake with her right hand only, her left gripping a bag of frozen peas. She mixes the rose water, oil and golden syrup with flour and lets it rest.

Some of her eggs rebel. They burst out of the shell, through cracks. She laughs at the little knobs and horn bubbles, and he notices. He has warned her.

"Are you crazy?" he asks. "Yes," she rolls her eyes. She has the moon on her side: Luna, lunatic, lunar catastrophe.

She's a kick-ass cook in any language. It's the *sinestra* thing. While everyone pays attention to the right hand, the lamb hand of the God who tested Abraham, she raises her cloven goat paw to snatch inspiration, a pinch of cardamom, a teaspoon of ginger and a pinch of stardust.

Words are for recipes, spells and prayer. They are the unsilent component. She wishes, not measuring, counts as she stirs, raps while she beats, chants while she pours, quotes Shakespeare and Donne during foreplay, sometimes e e cummings, "No one, not even the rain has such small hands." The ear is an erotic zone. When will they learn? He plays her like a stringed instrument, lots of arpeggios, then she sings. She is, after all a poet.

What is a lost credit card compared to a stunning haiku, the "Maison d'or" duet from *The Pearl Fishers* played on his guitar, a perfect moon cake filled with lotus seed paste or a beautiful orgasm, lotus petals opening on a starlit lake, when the moon is full?

She considers fully submerging the antique eggbeater, a major no-no. Recently, after a tiff, she emptied the dustpan in his omelette. Oops.

They call it rude hour, after her info-crush, the silver-haired CNN anchor, reads the evening news, after bathing together in tepid water because he hates to be hot, after eating cake, their hunger exacerbated by dissonance, after he finds her new message folded in his perfect triangle of moon: REPENT.

Really? For what he might ask, but doesn't, except in his own mind-list of grievances for guarding what is his, what is hers by virtue of being his, for protecting her from her impulses, her carelessness, her broad strokes, from stolen credit cards and disfigured eggs, from rats in the year of the rat (many he has personally disposed of, catching them in traps in her deliberately overgrown garden of rampant ivy and clematis, bagging then taking them to a garbage can in the park so she won't have to see them when she disposes of their household waste), and from the squirrel who steals her gold-wrapped ginger candies and buries them in the garden, "Don't leave the doors and windows open!" Who is the one to apologise? Who actually requires a festival to justify her womanhood, her own personal lady-moon?

She gets in bed first, watches through the bathroom portal while he performs oral hygiene, the floss, the toothpick, the slow and thorough brushing; watches him clean his glasses, wind the clock, set the clock; watches him carefully fold his clothes, fit shoehorns in his ugly-ass Bruno Maglis, torn from the body of a deceased tycoon and sold to him for a song at Value Village; watches him turn out the lights, wishes she too could pass wind at will, and wonders if that extra piece of moon cake is slowly inflating his belly, if it will lead to the cardiac event she fears more than anything. She wants to put her finger down his throat.

Someone turns the moonlight on.

He watches her watching him. She says she is invisible, but she isn't. He tells her, but she doesn't believe him, that he embraces her pillow when she gets up first, that he sniffs her clothes hanging in the closet, her shoes, her handbags, that he actually likes her decomposing skin, "Patina!"

She was programmed to imbibe negativity in the time when men hated intelligent women, when men had opinions and opinionated women were bitches. Is it not still that time? She has after all noticed ruthless exercise, inflated lips and brows, frozen faces. Viral insecurity.

"Don't speak!" Who knew that Garbo, reportedly an androgyne, was speaking to herself, that Garbo was afraid of bells because she was stung by bees sleeping in a bell she'd inadvertently rung.

Just the other night, because she had meant to walk but gave in to her fear of the dark, she got on a late bus after a poetry reading and told him when she arrived home that a man had changed seats three times to be near her. "I would be remiss," the man said when she pressed the buzzer for her stop, "if I didn't tell you I found you incredibly attractive." If she'd remembered her glasses, she could have told him what the man looked like. There's no point in fabricating. He knows all the indicators. She flutters her lids when she's lying. She over-describes and takes gulps of air.

"I hid behind a tree in case he followed, wondering if you would come out to look for me."

"You are the psychic, the intuitive one. I thought you'd visualised someone to drive you home."

"It doesn't work that way."

In fact, she saw the pride in his eyes. Mine, he thought, an old girl someone desired. She liked that, but as happens all too often, fell asleep before they could capitalize on the moment, another ritual. She is turned on by his music, by women rattling their bracelets in praise, leaving their chairs damp.

"Don't hurt our love," he says for the thousandth time, since the first time. They have many rituals: the coffee ritual, the buffing their wedding rings ritual, the gathering eggs ritual, the speaking crow on the roof ritual, the share the chocolate ritual and the rude hour ritual, where the unspeakable is spoken. Now it is rude hour....

...and, this is how they make up, lying in bed, naked as jays, holding hands, reciting their unholy canticles, four-letter words for body emissions, trumpet involuntary. "Fart," he says, "Puss," she says." Come, "he says, "Tear," she says, "Pooh," he says, "Milk," she says, her trump card. She is a mother. Nothing trumps milk.

"Song," he says, already checked by her queen. "Poem," she replies, there are no songs without words, not really, and starts purring, no snoring—her prerogative. He leans over and plants one on the back of her neck, because she reacts like a cat when he nibbles her there.

"Kiss checks word," a dead poet whispers in her sleep. She doesn't give the poem tiptoeing through her body another thought.

SHADOW DANCING

I don't know any of these people. What to bring? Is beer too plebeian, wine too chic? Maybe they drink *kava*? Not me, I had an allergic reaction, sick for days after I drank the green muck at an old hippy birthday at a Sonoma vineyard, the one where my husband and Dan Hicks, dead now, pouted in the shade and blew their last chance to play together, old buddies, while the hosts danced to an alien salsa band, because the birthday boy had at last acceded to his wife's beautiful longing to dance.

We have brought brownies, but not the Alice B. Toklas kind, another sick inducer. I went into a deep well for three days when someone surprised me with psychedelic icing at a Halloween party a few years ago. My brownies are from an online recipe, only I was missing an ingredient, cocoa, so I mixed chocolate chips with molasses and some maple syrup for the hell of it. My husband says they will not pass with old stoners.

The guests are wandering around dancing to silence, maybe to the angel band, I guess. I am so unhip. I introduce myself. No one else does it. These ghosts, parents of Saffron, Sage, Stinging Nettle et al., are a cornucopia of edible plants from the safe side of Paradise—no Cains or Abels, and all appear to answer to plain names like Jane, Bob, Jack and Susan. It's Bob's birthday, and they have gathered from the parameters of affluence, discreetly parking their Mercedes down the street as if they might have ridden in on donkeys or walked the yellow brick road to Bob's house, resplendent in their iconoclast uniforms, sandals and love beads, bearing the geriatric hippy versions of frankincense and myrrh, bundles of hash and virtuous bread.

There is an undercurrent. Bob's house, a large Arts and Crafts cottage in Oak Bay, is apparently contentious. She left. He stayed. The second Bob Wife hunkers down in the kitchen making quinoa salads. She is the thin one, wearing, because this is a sixties party, lace hipsters that show off her suntanned legs and a short leather top with a fringe covering a paucity of mammalian infrastructure. I help put out the food. She says, when asked, that she is childless, a free spirit. She doesn't appear to have cooked a lot. Her fringe keeps getting in the food. Second Bob Wife keeps flicking it away. The flicks could be stardust in the dying light, wasted particles of the universe.

Meanwhile First Wife, a much larger woman, perhaps unhappy in her new relationship and secretly gorging on her allegedly legendary deep-fried ginger tofu, is pissing on everything that was theirs, now all his or New Theirs. "We bought this in the Kadiköy antique market."

She is showing off the light fixture in the dining room, a Byzantine variation on Mackintosh with descending amber bulbs, and she actually lifts her cobalt silver-blue Afghan skirt, an ethnic dress that cost a small fortune at Sunny Goodge Street (Rumour has it there were third world people working the sewing machines and knitting over the shop) to polish the brass switch plate where the lamp turns on.

"Oooo," we say. "How could you leave that behind?"

How indeed? There are many familiar objects. The guests point this way and that. "Remember," they say, and New Wife actually cuts her finger. Her blood mixes in with the before-mentioned flicks because she can't miss a beat. If she does, nothing will get done, and besides it looks as if she might implode. No one else is helping. Everyone else is busy admiring the old stuff, telling the war stories attached to acquiring the old stuff, the memories she may or may not be a part of.

Or perhaps they were best friends, and they traded. *Bob and Carol, Ted and Alice.* That happened a lot after someone started passing around a copy of *Open Marriage.*

My only experience with that was waking up in the middle of the night to find Someone's Wife in our tent where Someone had dumped her during a camping trip. Apparently, he had suggested I join him, but I missed it because I am a deep sleeper, then as now. Lucky me.

Somehow I don't think my extemporaneous fantasy is working. There isn't that old-friend familiarity between the two women, the affection that suggests former threesomes, or foursomes, keys on the coffee table, shared joints, pots of tea and placenta helper, that sort of thing.

These are not my people, the marriage is forever, study hard, say no to drugs kind of people. They are party people on the cusp of, oboy, prune mixed with sedatives, the new party in your mouth. I smugly recall the dementia people I know are all former drug users, mostly mother's little helpers, the amphetamines that kept our mothers skinny and busy in the fifties. Now it is our turn, love-in ingestibles and injectibles having the last word.

When I drift from the kitchen to the sunroom, I realise my husband has opted not to socialise. He has two options at ill-fitting parties. One is to hang around the food and eat his face off, which I worry will lead to a coronary event, and the other is to pick like a deranged Latvian. Tonight it is option two, and I opt to listen so I don't have to listen. Conversation between hard-of-hearing strangers is exhausting, and I will save that chore for the almost inevitable out-to-pasture warehousing, the option I am trying desperately to avoid.

Luke is singing "The Snake," redeeming the song written by civil rights activist Oscar Brown and twisted by the Mango Surprise (not so much) at campaign rallies, transforming refugees from Amerika's Imperial Wars into brown Satans.

Way to go, human beings. We are all force-dancing with the devil now. Dignified death and what to be next have become major obsessions. I am thinking of Cocaine with Chinese poison and tree burial.

I like the idea of becoming a tree, as opposed to a diamond ring (Is it vulgar? Who would wear me?) but am not sure what kind of tree I want to be. Would I be evergreen or deciduous? Should I bear fruit, or nuts? My children would agree with the nut option. I can just hear them. "That's appropriate," they would say in unison, an opinion substantiated by going through my stuff, a lifetime of oddities. Maybe I will be a pine. I like the smell, nothing like the pine forest on the road from Izmir to Cesme.

The party guests are not focused on death. No one mentions the absent friends. No one mentions the fame and fortune that eluded them, just the starlit moments when they actually met someone famous or handled his old guitar in a consignment shop. Names are dropping like turds at the dog park.

"This was Joan's. Mimi let me play it." Because I have been around, I can translate. Joan Baez, guilty about her fortune, twinned every purchase and gave one to her friends, who sometimes consigned them. We've seen lots of dresses we recognize in thrift shops. My husband is expert at culling ordinary *shmatte* from *haute couture.*

I arrange myself by the fireplace, shirts fanned out, ankles crossed, expression unassailable, neither bored nor socially anxious, enduring the overly familiar music in a chair upholstered in velvet. These people live in the suburbs of fame and fortune. It's just that I have never heard of them.

"That's a beautiful dress," he hands me his card while I look for traces of hair under the red cowboy kerchief tied, Hell's Angel style, around his pate. The grey braids could be fake.

"Thanks. It was designed by Gareth Helter in the sixties." I say this as if he is supposed to know Gareth Helter. I looked him up after finding the dress in a new-to-you.

"Oh yeah. What happened to him?"

"He died of AIDS in the eighties."

"Didn't everyone?" He has that dreamy stupid look of a guy who can't go to a party without getting stoned first.

"No not all." I am feeling bitchy and alive. "Some of us have been lucky, if you call witnessing the downfall of the American Empire a good view."

This is way too many words for him. His "country" kerchief could be a red flag. He adjusts his headscarf, licks his lips and reaches in the inside pocket of his Afghan vest lined with sheepskin, which must be hot.

"Can I give you my card?"

This is cute. Does he want me to buy his product, probably a self-published album, or should I be calling him for a noon assignation, white wine and bed salad, culminating in the inevitable erectile failure and the usual excuses, "I'm upset by your stretch marks," "You weren't ready for me" and the best one of all, "Your hearing aids are a real turnoff?"

"I'll give it to my husband. He's younger than I am, and he reads small print better," I say, tucking it in my *banca abuela,* the granny bank named by my granddaughter when I tucked the tourist pesos, *cucs*, between my, trust me, still perky breasts.

At the word, the warning, he turns tail. I know doctors who keep photos of dead wives and grown children front and centre on their desks to discourage patients who think because he or she has had their hands on them that must be a bond. "Husband" works too. Mine gets up and leans into me. "Do you know who that is?"

"No, and I don't want to." I return to my resting bitch face.

I know the other women are watching, but they do not react. I still call it the Mean Girl expression. Maybe I am missing something in their body language, a blink, or muscle spasm. Why not me, some might be thinking, or why is he still trying, or I can't believe he's still using the cards.

We will not be bonding, the "me" I brought to the party and these people. I am not of them, even though I did skinny-dip with the hippy who married the Prime Minister on the night of the moon-landing. I did not share specular views when that was fashionable, when knowing your vagina and your girlfriends' vaginas was essential to modernity, or clay strained relics from playschool, a recent meme.

I am actually invisible to all but my husband and bandana man, Willie's twin, who reeks of desperation. I get it. Loneliness is what happens, even if, especially if, there were times when life was defined by a crowd function beyond imagining, surging audiences overtaking stages like waves and bands of groupies waiting backstage. It takes a while to figure out that fans are not friends. These are things I have not had to resolve because I am an observer. These things are obvious when you are watching.

I was tempted to clap when he spun away from me with a small theatrical shrug. He kept his back straight and avoided eye contact, engaging the next woman, who appeared to be enthralled. It is performance. I have seen if before, men who try and try as if trying were their masculine imperative, and maybe it is. Roosters affect indifference when they troll the barnyard delivering little squirts here and there, as do the hens that are simply about the business of laying eggs with little haemorrhages in the yolks, proof of life.

That's it. These guys are all roosters. They never give up, and we, the girls in the room, are still girls. I am not sure I want this to be an end-of-life revelation, the result of years of feminist activism.

I am now remembering a time before I met my husband, when I was insulted, no deeply hurt, by an interim lover who told me my inability to have more children meant I was no longer a woman. Never mind that I had delivered dead babies in the middle of the night, into a dark and terrible loneliness. Never mind that my surviving children struggled to live, that I struggled with them and the failure of my husband to share it with me meant the end of a family I intended to honour. Did that make me less a woman?

I stood up in the patio bar on St. Denis where all his friends were celebrating the beginning of *le weekend* and tore my dress from the neck to the waist, revealing my breasts. I walked out, and he followed, frantically trying to cover me with his Armani jacket. "You are mad," he said.

"Yes," I said, "as in angry," not crazy. I knew what I was doing.

I am mad now, not crazy but angry that a man testing his power would try to pick me up, especially in front of my husband, that he would think his row of Junos gave him the right to try. Mad that he fails to see I am more than just a dress, that I too have backstory and a credible vocation. Mad that other women are watching. Mad that he would try again, and mad that we have all endured the systemic misogyny of the recent American election, where the only qualified candidate was too old to fuck.

My husband is back in his chair singing "Down Home Girl," possibly because he sees me smouldering, and he knows I love the song. I know what to do. I fix my eyes on bandana man and slowly take over the middle of the room. The dancers back off. It is all quiet except for my husband's voice.

Every time you monkey child
Takes my breath away.
Every time you move like that
Girl I got to get down and pray.

First I take off my shoes and then my earrings and bracelets. Then comes the dress, which I pull over my head and swing like a matador's cape. Now I will step out of my underpants. I give them a moment to take that in and then do it. I am as naked as the day I entered the world backwards, bum first and left-handed, *sinestra,* as brave as Nicole Kidman in *The Killing of the Sacred Deer,* no braver, because she's as thin as a whip. My blog nom de plum is Sinestra Libtard. You may have seen it. I take no prisoners.

I raise my arms and bounce in place. My breasts rise and fall. I suck the air out of the room, and my husband stops singing.

I let it sink in, and then I swoop to pick up my things. It is time to leave. I signal to my husband, put away your instrument. Now. My well-rehearsed non-negotiable look. Get. Me. Out. Of. Here. I dress, or re-dress, and we collect the untouched uncool brownie plate and our various appointments: glasses, purse, mandolin and knitting bag, and head for the door.

On the threshold, I look back. The guests are all our age, from another time. I think Rolling Stones, a band of beef jerky dressed like happy children. This is the zombie jamboree, none of them still alive in the way they were, twitching to the music, decapitated chickens.

Robin is singing "Devil in a Blue Dress." Good for him. First Wife smiles her deranged smile, gets up and begins to dance, her silver-blue skirts swirling around her.

Got to be the finest girl alive
She got such good lovin' that
they cannot say goodbye.

She is truly in her body. Arms raised, waving like octopus tentacles, she spins around the bobbers, pushing them back to the perimeters of the room where she lay several times on a mattress and gave birth while they watched and marvelled about the miracle of life, and once death because the cord was wrapped around the baby's neck and they were too stoned to react. This is their bond. This is their journey, from start to finish.

My husband and I back out the door. I am a stranger. He is a stranger. We look at one another and smile. Our smiles are for the First Wife. Her shadow dances on the walls. She owns the room. She always did.

BEDTIME STORIES

So that's it!" Kiss Man, my permanent attachment, led me into a grass-covered square of light in the woods, a majestic stand of cedars smelling of bark scars, sap and damp leaves, with a picnic, a blanket and his fiddle, and made the Earth move. I wonder if any girl has ever been more surprised by lust than I was that afternoon, when after sup and sip, a murder of crows tangled wings, a *frisson,* in the yellow-taped crime zone between my legs.

I had scars from inappropriate touching. Invisible wounds. When I fell off my bicycle and scraped my knees, I ate the scabs. My cannibal snacks gave me immunity to falling, better balance. Ditto to sexual assault. I thought I was immune to carnal love.

"No thanks," I'd said to grappling boys, their confidence fuelled by cherry cokes, as I ate my way out of the candy store.

However, there is a back door to everything, one portal I'd missed, possibly because it is the front door to infinite pleasure.

"How about dessert?" he began to play Mendelssohn,

Jewish courtship. I felt ravens brushing my thighs with their feathers, calling my name, my first little death, a joke. I got it.

The grass-shaped square of light trembled.

So this was why my father locked himself in his library with his long-playing records and a bottle of whiskey, "Eine Kleine Nachtmusic," sexy-time. I was genetically programmed for musical foreplay. After Mendelssohn, it was "Mysterious Barricades" and how mine fell. I rolled backwards, and it rained light, exploding sequins, iridescent notes.

Back in the days of grinding boys and driving beats, I'd shut the door on music. But now it opened both ways; and there was no more playing with silence, Rostropovich's mute broom handle, his first instrument. I dusted off my child-sized cello and practiced every erotic piece of music in the known universe: Messiaen's "Joie du sang des étoiles," Scriabin's "Poème de l'extase," Tristan and Isolde's "Liebesnacht," the sound of boots knocking in the Black Forest, with little breaks for *mes petites morts*.

With him, I discovered minor keys, dark notes, sotto voce, the earthquake zone, rhapsodic chords with crashing cymbals, I had never imagined. We were bread and butter, salt and pepper, surprise, a duo.

We rubbed bows in private, two happy grasshoppers "fucking with music." "Let's fuck with music," he insisted, and we did, foreplay for what we call "The Infidelity Game," pillow talk.

Last night, it was his turn. He confessed that my former best friend stalked him for years, secretly went to my hairdresser for my haircut and bought clothes that matched mine, a magenta angora sweater for one, unmistakable, turned up in men's washrooms (accidents, she's high functioning on the scale and doesn't get jokes), sniffing under the table at dinner parties (She was always losing her earrings. He thought it was the dog.) and digging deep for the popcorn at movies, the third party: one, two, three in a row, girl, boy, girl. I remember mentioning his beard tasted odd one morning. It was, he now tells me, the morning after she climbed in our bedroom window at midnight and, singing an Italian art song, sat on his face. "Caro mio ben," is not a particularly original choice, but she's a soprano not a rocket scientist. He woke up. I did not.

Did I remember seeing her ladder?

One of the rules is that we are not allowed to say whether a story is made up or not. It is up to the other to guess, true or false. Truth or fiction, there is always a troubling equivocal detail. This story could be true. I wear earplugs because he snores. She might have left the ladder there. He didn't want to spoil our friendship.

"False," I said.

"Wrong," he answered, fishing, and I consciously choose that word, a pair of foreign bikini underpants from the dream stash under his pillow.

But of course, he could have stolen them off a clothesline.

"You go," he says, tonight being my turn somewhere in the middle of a thousand and one nights. "Tell."

"Do you want funny or sad?" I ask, mopping up after an unorthodox "Rhapsody in Blue." We keep tissues in every room, just in case the muse captures us unaware.

"Both," he says. He is an omnivore. "Tell me about the threesome in Bath. We never got to that one."

"OK, and what are we wagering?"

"Dinner at Brasserie L'école?"

"Sure. I want steak frites and a really nice cab, *Burrowing Owl* for example."

"You always have whatever your heart desires."

"Don't I know it?"

"Begin."

I close my eyes and try to remember exactly how it happened, or not. The problem with being a storyteller is that, after several repeats, it is hard to distinguish between real and imagined.

"It was the last time I visited Ruth in London. You had that gig in Berlin. We were having tea in the aerie at the British Museum, a tower of petites fours, lemon tarts and scones with champagne and tea."

"That tea cost a fortune."

"You were not supposed to look at the bill. Now, shhh, listen or I will lose my place."

"Ruth loves to play head games. 'Will you take a dare?' she asked."

"Depends." For one thing, I wasn't going to take off my dress and walk naked down the marble stairs to the enormous public hall downstairs.

"How about if I offered you a thousand pounds to play 'Kol Nidre,' the Aramaic prayer of atonement?"

"In a synagogue?" It made sense. It was fall, the right time of year.

"No, this is a private performance, and you'll have to go to Bath."

"Well I can't. I don't have an instrument."

"They will take care of that."

"Who is 'They'?"

"Not telling."

"A thousand pounds?"

"That's right, plus travel. You can take the train."

"Would I come out of this alive? Is this a murderer atoning for his sins and possibly getting ready to commit the next one?"

"We are all murderers or accomplices. We eat meat don't we? I will give you a clue. It is about sex and death and don't forget that Charles and Patricia Lester dress you wanted at Liberty's."

My mind went back to our picnic in the woods. I closed my eyes to think, and I saw myself feeding crows in a Lester pleated silk dress. So I agreed.

"The next day, I wore white as requested, and Ruth dropped me at Euston Station. 'Pray for me,' I ordered, and she giggled, handing me a bag from Marks and Spencer's, ham and cheese in a bun as it turned out. I was too nervous to eat the sandwich, but I did buy a beer on the train."

"When I arrived, a chauffeur carrying a cardboard sign with my name on it was waiting at the station. It wasn't far. No distance would have been far enough. The streets in Bath all looked the same, tidy, symmetrical, unlike my unraveling life, or so I imagined. The familiar musical feeling, a coochie smile, reminded me that fear and sex lurk in the same abyss. If it hadn't been for the Lester dress, I would have had the driver turn around and take me back to the train."

"After we arrived at a Georgian house like every other on the street, an elderly butler opened the door into a marble hall, veered left, led me into a conservatory filled with lilies and asked me to sit on a green velvet occasional chair placed a man's length away from a matching chaise longue. I took in my surroundings and tried not to pass out in the scented heat while a maid served tea and poppy seed cookies."

"She said the tea was 'Emperor's Tears.' I suppose it was to put me in the right frame for playing the 'Kol Nidre.' The conservatory was uncomfortably warm, especially as I was wearing a wool dress, and the smell of lilies was suffocating. I made myself swallow a biscuit and several sips of tea. Eventually the butler returned carrying a cello case, which he laid against the chaise longue, and told me to take the instrument out, to be ready to play, but not to speak. Then he took away the tray."

"Was the tea drugged?" he asks.

"Stop interrupting. I mean it. You will have to forfeit the prize."

"You always make me pay," he says. "What's the difference?"

"I took the cello, an Amati, out of its case and tuned it, then sat and breathed in and out with the lilies. I thought they sighed."

"After many expirations of plant breath, the owner of the house, a thirtyish man who could have been plucked from a pre-Raphaelite painting came into the conservatory wearing a maroon dressing gown. He was carrying a life-sized bride doll bundled in silk and net, which he laid on the chaise, and followed by a large yellowish hound."

"Was the bride a Japanese inflatable with French braided pubic hair?"

"Goddammit. I am going to smother you with your pillow."

"Look out for dirty underpants."

"Without speaking to me, or even acknowledging my presence, the man began to undress his flaccid bride, first the bodice, which he unbuttoned slowly, covering her bosom with kisses. There was no cue, but I assumed this was where I should play."

"Since Ruth paid half my fee in advance, before I left London, I could have got up and left. But I didn't. I was transfixed."

"In the beginning, I tried not to look, but eventually I did, and I could see that this bride might not be a doll. She could have been a corpse, or someone drugged to resemble death, like Juliet. Trust me, my back hair stood up. My teeth chattered. My blood froze."

"And your meat curtain rose."

"You bugger interrupter."

"Of course it did."

"The bride was wearing nothing but her peau de soie dress, no petticoat, no other underwear. There were no marks on her that I could see. Either she was drugged or he had killed her. Maybe she was a suicide, dead on her wedding day. Maybe she loved someone else."

"I decided to play for her, not him."

"She must have heard, because her soul got up and stood behind me. I felt her cold dead hands brush my shoulders. The *frisson* made my bow shiver."

"Meanwhile he took off her wedding slippers and kissed each white foot in turn. Then he removed her veil, and I saw her features properly. She was neither smiling nor unhappy. Her face looked indifferent. He undid her long black hair, which had been held in place with pearl ornaments, and covered her body with it. Then he lay down on top of his passive bride and made love to her."

"I kept playing. The hound howled. He actually knew the tune."

"Electric impulses jolted my nipples and groin. Averting my eyes again, I played until he finished, and looked up when he came, raising his arms in the air gasping like a great bird then sinking down on her, losing himself in her hair."

"The bridegroom ignored me, speaking only to his bride, while the butler brought in another tray, just for them. He got on his knees and fed his doll bride sips of tea, which dribbled down her chin and into the little lake of tears at the base of her neck, begging her to taste a piece of wedding cake wrapped in a napkin on a china plate. Then he put it under her pillow. "Sweet dreams," he said.

"All the while, I played and the dog howled. When the song was finished, he picked her up and carried her out. The hound stayed."

"So this was atonement."

"The dog swallowed my ham and cheese sandwich in one gulp. He left tooth marks on my hand. That was the grace bite. I couldn't get out of there fast enough."

"I put the cello back in its case, stood up, backed to the marble hall saying 'nice doggie,' and found a powder room where I washed and washed my hands and wrapped the injured hand in a monogrammed hand towel, which I kept. The butler then saw me to the door and handed me an envelope, which I was not about to open in front of him. The event in itself was humiliating enough. I am sure the manservant, lurking somewhere behind the flowers, had heard my gasps of pleasure as I played."

"A terrible noise came from an upstairs room with an open window: my employer sobbing, the dog caterwauling and the one word, 'Lily!' so intense I heard it all the way out to the street, where my driver waited."

"I got in and laughed hysterically all the way to the train station. I couldn't help myself, unaccustomed as I am to playing Jewish laments for mad dogs and perverted English aristocrats. The driver gave me a handkerchief that smelled of lavender, and I opened the envelope containing the balance with a generous tip and a note saying, 'There is no greater agony than love' written in green ink."

"Do you think that green ink was his blood?"

"How would I know? Maybe it was hers, plus formaldehyde. Aren't aristocrats supposed to have blue blood?"

"What did Ruth say when you got back to London?"

"She asked me how it went."

"And you told her everything, including your response?"

"Of course. She said it was some sort of ritual initiation. All the new string players in her orchestra are given challenges."

"What happens if they refuse?"

"I have no idea. She took me out to a pub for dinner with the string section that night, and there were lots of jokes and toasts. I think they had all done it."

"With the same dead body?"

"Well, maybe it *was* a doll."

"Or perfect embalming. Or actors."

"Ooo creepy. I wonder who pays?"

"No idea."

"Why didn't you tell me?"

"I'm telling you now."

"We're both good at keeping secrets."

"And lies."

"Now it is time to guess." I can feel his little buddy nudging my backside.

"OK."

"I say false. I think you slipped up on the living or dead detail."

"You lose. Want to see the scar on my wrist?"

"Wasn't that from the Thanksgiving your father kissed the au pair girl while your mother was carving the turkey and you got between them?"

"That's another story. You pay this time."

NESTING

We call it nesting. Woolgathering and phenomenal collection: memories, songs, sticks and feathers, yes, a nest.

This evening, you added one more, hung your new painting in the only wall space left, over the bathtub, a hybrid collision of *Le printemps* with *Guernica*, exploding blossoms in the foreground, black storm in the background.

I've turned down the bed, run the bath, poured in lavender oil and lit the candles.

We get in, hopefully to relax, admire the view, the new landscape, a *vernissage*, and our garden filled with birds settling down to rest.

"Is that smoke?" I ask, pointing to the dark cloud in the painting. It's hard to see in candlelight.

"No, it's blackbirds."

"Ahhhh." Our jazz combo, birds on the telephone wire swagged in the trees in front of our house, is already asleep.

When the water cools, we step out, shake, turn out the lights and feel our way to bed, operating on instinct, navigating our inessential necessities, sometimes stumbling because we are flawed species, male and female.

"Scratch please," I ask when we get into bed. Our ritual.

And you do, then we kiss, more of a peck, the disappearing lips, and turn to sleep, welcome the pair of enchanting smooth groove roller skaters who invited themselves into our dreams after we saw them perform on YouTube.

We call it brain TV, and we can't or won't turn them off, the picture anyway.

The soundtrack is anyone's guess. Unlike the dance, it segues into morning.

Sometimes it's faint, sometimes silent. Could be Ella and Duke on the radio, but the real music is a man and woman skating backwards, into the radiant arch, our arms lifted up to make a bridge, first couple in the country dance, London Bridge, sometimes safe for lovers.

The roller skaters barely touch, just a nudge, hips and knees, the right way to ride a horse, with signals, equestrian dancing but not dressage, no reins and bits, no cruel drool, just a beautiful ride to the shining city on the hill. Rapture.

It don't mean a thing/ if you ain't got that swing

The smooth groove skaters cross step, never trip. It helps that their feet turn in. Pigeon toes are their secret ingredient. They float, no wind resistance, arms held out for balance, moving the air like swimmers in pools of pure oxygen.

We are touch navigators too.

There's no moon tonight. We fly blind in synchronized sleep, feet tangled, top sheet untucked, winding us as we turn and turn while the smooth groove skaters keep on rolling, rock and roll, thank you Mister Domino, maintaining the gospel bounce, steps in sync, wings lifting.

Blackbird singing in the dead of night
Take these broken wings and learn to fly.
All your life, you were only waiting for
this moment to arise.

The film loops and loops, and I'm wondering about morning, the sound of wheels rolling in perfect unison, the static, the beat, our crowfriends warming up the frozen telephone wires outside our bedroom window, dancing and defecating, messaging, the crow thing, their aubade, words and music. Scat. Thaw. Hello crow. Can you hear me? I hear you. Will we be alive again?

Put on those red shoes and run away from the blues.

It's all good. We stay with the rogue dream and the rogue top sheet, sex and death, and isn't jazz derived from *jism*, jelly roll with or without a marriage license, feathers flying? We ask the crows, and they always answer. Yes, to clicks, rattles and coos; yes, to the message in drumming and tap dancing, hearts beating in unison, unmade beds, juke jam. Yes.

I roll over and sniff your chest, jasmine, my own perfume, scent of Paradise, the Persian word for enclosed gardens, winter in Havana, summer in Izmir, plants on the porch in summer, rooms in winter, so many rooms, so many beds and the constants, cats at night, blackbirds and doves in the morning. All that jazz. Cu-ckoo, the slang for pussy in Istanbul.

I'm still here, somewhere between asleep and awake, anticipating the world view, bird's-eye view, but not quite ready to end this dream, but you stir first, unwind the sheet, preen your feathers.

Are we going somewhere today?

Our smooth groove skaters fade into their glory hole, but the crows keep rocking the wire outside our bedroom window

"Boogie Woogie's a disease," you say, laughing as usual, pulling me into a column of light surrounded by blackbirds. We're fully-fledged, dressed for success.

"Lift off," you say. "Rise and shine!"

If I was a blackbird, I'd pack my troubles on my back.
I would leave this world, and I never would look back.

LUCY LAUGHED

I met her at a gallery opening, his. Once a year, in revolving seasons, Liam and Lucy travel to Madagascar, where he paints lemurs and she studies lemur behaviour. Her books, cover art by him, were on sale at his show.

The gallery was packed, and the crowd nudged me into the personal zone, nose to nose with Liam's creatures. His impasto was so compelling I wanted to touch it, to pat the fur, scratch behind the ears. Sometimes we cross boundaries. Sometimes we are seen doing the wrong thing. Last year, I set off an alarm when I got too close to Van Gogh's feverish sunflowers at the Tate. Lucy's alarm went off when a lemur hand reached out of the canvas to grab mine. She startled.

"Sorry," I apologized.

"Don't be," she said. "It's a compliment. You must be from the same cohort."

CLUE, my brain should have signalled, but it didn't. We laughed, and then I told her about watching a toddler in the virtual generation attempt to climb inside a computer frame and curl up with the kittens inside.

"We all need to sleep in piles," she agreed.

"I know," I said, "where the wild things are!" and Lucy nodded.

I know about lemurs but not as much as Lucy, clearly warmed up by my enthusiasm. Lemurs are adorable, and endangered, chased to Madagascar by the first Diaspora and thereafter hunted by humans.

"You probably know the Romans thought they were ghosts," I stopped there because, of course she knows and competitive pedantry is boring. Besides, I am at the age when nobody cares what I think. Time to put a cork in it.

Lucy is a little outside the zone herself, could be a lady lemur with her kohl eyes.

"Your hair is stunning," I observed, circumventing blurts about her primate makeup, tattooed eyeliner and lipstick, focusing instead on her luxuriant mane, which danced like Disney princess hair, to her waist.

"Liam grooms it," she answered, and my eyes swerved from her self-touching to a painting of two lemurs picking one another's nits.

"I don't have cooties, but he's a mean man with a brush," she laughed, an unforgettable sound.

"Clearly."

"Did you know that 'gossip' started as 'God's sip,' woman talk during community nitpicking sessions?"

"No," I lied, crossing my fingers discretely around the stem of my cocktail glass; but I think she was smart enough to see I was being disingenuous to get her to talk. Chat is my Internet. Her eyes narrowed ever so slightly when I told her I'd missed the gossip story at Sunday School. In fact I was a prize-gathering star at Sunday School, partly because I had a comic book Bible, Old and New Testament, and couldn't resist the uncensored stories of lust and vengeance, with paradisiacal bookends, truth and reconciliation, forgiveness.

She's an anthropologist, and gossip is an anthropologist's gospel. Maybe that is why my mother boasted about sleeping with Margaret Mead after she had helped Mead out of her girdle at a conference on sexual norms, where they were both giving papers. My mother's lecture was on women in art. Mead's was on devolving primate orthodoxies.

I knew I'd be telling Lucy this story when I got to know her better. Apparently Mead travelled with a photo of her ex-husband, and my mother woke up from a post-coital nap to find the castoff staring at her. She dined out on the story for years. Every time I heard it, I reminded myself that she'd thrown darts at a portrait she'd done of my father when she was still in lust with him.

Yes, I knew about God's sip. I am after all, curious, and we all, all but sociopaths, need stories to justify our desperate behaviour, outrunning mothers with darts.

"When lemurs are extinct, we will still have Liam's paintings," Lucy said, as if reading then translating my thoughts. I must be transparent in my glass hat, like those thought-revealing Leakey sculptures at the Victoria and Albert Museum.

"Why don't you come to our fruitcake tasting party

next Sunday afternoon? I'll show you his studio."

"Fruitcake?" Would I have to be certified to get past the butler?

I am an art dealer's dream. Certain words, certain phrases fire my endorphins, my insatiable hunger for information and acquisition, and drain my savings. "My studio" is one of them, and "tasting" is another. An art historian, driven by curiosity, I know how medieval painters laid down their gold leaf and their models, how they got the virtuous Marys and St. Annes to show their nipples. I know how to pounce a cartoon in gesso and how to pounce on a story.

I smelled the nutmeg. Lucy, who looks as if she could be Liam's transmogrified model, threw an antique finish over a surreal overture.

"Wear your furs. We keep the heat down."

I was at once intrigued and repelled by this possible joke. Surely Liam and Lucy are animal conservationists? Once again, she read the sand moving through my mind, and laughed. How to describe the sound? Picture a leash of bucks in space shaking their belled antlers in unison. Irresistible. Fruitcake. Resistible. Fat and salt are my food groups.

This is the appointed day. I take care to dress like an adult primate, brown velvet and my mother's old sable coat with high-heeled crocodile boots. I don't wear new furs; only animals that died before I developed a conscience. I am anxious to engage Lucy in a conversation about possession by animal spirits.

In Oak Bay, where Liam and Lucy live, activism is chic. Power lines are buried underground, grocery stores are organic, and activists as brave as the Palestinians who put themselves between Israeli bulldozers and ancient olive groves stand in the rain to defend the Garry oaks from developers.

Liam and Lucy have put up an off-putting sign telling their guests to park in the field at the bottom of the hill to their house. I'm wearing my ridiculous boots, and the driveway is a quagmire. Only last week, I lost my bearings, walked into a pile of canine droppings and had to sacrifice a favourite pair of satin pumps. Nevertheless, curiosity rules, so I remove my ankle breakers, and brave the squishy moss and whatever vermin lives in the gravel, which is ice-cold, sharp and really unpleasant to step on.

My inquisitive spirit has taken me to some dark places, but I am determined this will not be one of them, in spite of the mud oozing between my toes. I reach the summit out of breath and put my boots back on when the driveway levels and circles around the house. Lucy watches, then strikes.

"Shoes off!" she sings from the top of the stairs, and I consider sliding down the driveway on the gluteus sled God gave me. Instead I comply. On my way to sleep tonight, I will imagine rapturous and discrete couplings between the microbes that live in her rugs and those on my stocking feet.

“Sorry, I didn’t bring slippers,” I apologise, but I’m really thinking about ways I might hide my ugly feet. As a ballet-mad teenager, I danced my way to deformity.

“Never mind,” Lucy says, shaking my hand with her left and caressing my sleeve with her right. “Oh, soft. Leave your coat in the green bedroom.”

Green, I find out, is the master bedroom, the walls painted with trees and predictably hung with Liam’s lemurs. I toss my coat in the heap on the bed. It poufs and drops with a sigh on top of the others, letting out the dogs and a top note of gardenia.

My mother wore Chanel Gardenia. Nothing else. No one else. She was quite singular, quite authentic and unabashedly hungry. Hunger without boundaries. I smelled gardenias on my pillow when I returned home after giving a class on Mannerism and the Counter-Reformation at Reed College and kicked my husband so hard he rolled out of the bed.

That was the end of my first marriage. My second husband told me my mother had just happened to walk across the sixteenth green stark naked while he was putting. That marriage lasted a little longer because I value honesty more than I despise golf.

When I return to Lucy in the hall, she’s greeting a man in a camel hair coat. He too is sent to green, and when he brushes by me, his sleeve feels as soft as baby rabbits. “Cashmere,” Lucy says, winking, then points to the drawing room, where an elderly Scottish woman in a maid’s uniform is serving tea.

Am I imagining she is the doppelganger for my nanny, who also had seven grey whiskers on her chin?

"Please, Scotty," I say, "You decide." She doesn't correct me, and I am hoping she will recognize me as the baby who wouldn't let go. There are dozens of cakes. "Heavy on the marzipan, please." One of my marriages lasted longer than it should because he liked fruitcake and I liked marzipan. We ate our way through dozens of weddings before we discovered our incompatibility.

Did I mention Scotch and tea?

She brings me a slice of something vibrant and tea infused with "Venus in Furs," and I am halfway to heaven after the first sip of silver moonlight with a salty finish. I am so happy with this flavour I don't at first notice that, with the exception of the help and myself, I am in a room full of men.

That calls for a second, and a third.

The odds are in my favour. I probably won't be driving myself home, and I can sample to my heart's content. I chat up a man who tells me he beads animal skulls. I ask if he kills them first and if his name also begins with the letter L.

"I'm Lewis," he says, gives me the look and remembers he needs to refresh his drink. After this happens several times, I wonder if I should spin the story that I am shod in chocolate socks, not mud. I could dip my toes in their bone china teacups. The room is thinning out.

This gives me a chance to study Liam's paintings, which are exquisitely tender. Like many magic realists, he prefers tempera. His animals are beautifully groomed, every brushstroke a caress. I've heard lemurs gather in troops like Girl Guides, but the proper collective noun for Liam's lemurs would be "a kindness."

Where is the promised atelier? I'm dying to see his work in progress.

The bearded nanny maid directs me to Liam's studio in the attic, access through the kitchen. I find the kitchen, break through a knot of cake nerds hanging around the cutting board and proceed upstairs, where the smell of turpentine is overwhelmed by something else, what my mother called jungle essence, but in plain talk is a mixture of sweat and tears with a top note of testosterone.

Liam is having an exchange with an art critic called Lloyd. Lloyd has had more than his measure of enhanced tea. I understand he is Welsh and should probably not mix his genres. What do the Welsh eat and drink? What makes them sing? Perhaps it is women like Lucy, who stands between them, giving out equal opportunity wrist slaps with her Chinese fan: one for Liam, one for Lloyd, as if they were children fighting over a toy.

"Mine," Liam shouts, rubbing his left hand in his right armpit and waving it about. Because I know my lemurs, I recognize this as a stink fight and for the sake of drama imagine the best man throwing Lucy over his shoulder and carrying her down to her boudoir. I worry about what will happen to my mother's coat.

The worst has happened before, when the sable was

new. My mother phoned me from a room in the Hotel Vancouver and told me a man she'd picked up at a meeting in the ballroom had made a mess of her coat, and as it was cold outside, I'd better send her another in a cab. Fifteen and hormonally nasty, I said, "Get him to buy you one, or stay there," and hung up.

The sable came home the next day, smelling of alcohol and vomit. Now it smells like dogs. The next time my mother went on one of her elected absences, I made it into a bed for our three King Charles spaniels.

I am sensitive to smells, and the stink fight makes me dizzy. I sit down on a wooden chair and put my head between my knees. All I can see are my feet, a swirling circle of toes and moss, and I am ashamed of them.

After my extreme body posture clears the room, I examine the paintings in progress, everything from bare gesso to cartoons, to nearly finished temperas. It's like watching progressive ultrasounds, growing foetuses thrashing and tumbling in the womb; only this time it's lemurs swimming from their island home in the new disapora.

What about us, I wonder. If it's sink or swim, will our fur coats make us buoyant or pull us down to the bottom of the sea from which we emerged with our superior intelligence? I'm voting for swim, because I am, in spite of everything, an optimist.

I go back downstairs to rejoin the human race, but except for nanny-maid banging dishes in the kitchen, all is quiet. The L people have vanished. I wander into the dining room and discover the most amazing arrangement of fruit: marzipan melons, pomegranates, grapes, figs, dates, apples and pears and lovely fruitcakes sliced and arranged on beautiful plates. I help myself to a branch of grapes and go exploring.

The door to the master bedroom is shut. I open it. "Hello?" I say, almost swallowing a grape.

The bed, piled with coats, moves and giggles.

"Hello?" then sounds like a leash of bucks shaking their belled antlers; or am I wrong, the laughter of ghosts playing hide and seek in dark rooms. Lemurs.

"Shhh," someone says, and the pile shifts on Liam and Lucy's queen-sized bed. "Come out, Mum." I hear myself saying, "Enough's enough."

THREE STRIKES

I like baseball. Three strikes and you're out. How clear is that—rules, cut and dried, a perfect covenant, *à la grisette,* Jonathon Swift's poeticized/satirized ho, a piece of jerky in her little grey dress?

And, thy beauty thus dispatch'd
Let me praise thy wit unmatch'd
Set of phrases, cut and dry
Evermore thy tongue supply.

My mind travels fast, faster than fastballs and agile tongues—from *grisette* to ball(s), ball to diamond, a song "Diamonds are a girl's best friend," and so on.

The first strike came though my editor's bay window, bevelled glass blasted to kingdom come, at least as far as the dining room and, as luck would have it, the kitchen, because the pantry door was open. It was a sunny afternoon. Light must have leaked through the broken window, and of course it refracted in the lethal bits that penetrated the Martha Stewart wallpaper and slipcovers and the oil painting of his mother, turning his living room into a veritable disco ball.

He never found the ball or the kid who threw or hit the ball, even though he ran directly outside, naked as it happens because he had just extricated himself from the shower. No kid, no ball, no mother dragging kid by the ear to apologize, no contacts. That would be four balls, a walk.

Because he prided himself on logic, he deduced from this lack of forensic information that the beautiful explosion in his living room was caused by a bullet. This is what he told the cops, "I was standing in the window (actually showing his wet/naked/fragrant, I'm leaving out steatopygous, self to the young Adonis drinking a gin and tonic on his porch across the street), and someone shot at me. Luckily he missed."

Did the cop smirk as he wrote this down in his book? Did he roll his eyes when a careful search failed to turn up bullets or balls of any description?

"Were you singing?" he asked, a leading question. This cop wants to be a lawyer and clearly likes to practice his clever-in-court theatricals. Windows break when the fat soprano sings.

No runs, no errors. Nothing. The cop left and he was alone with his fears, his undisciplined King Charles spaniel and a sideboard full of expensive distillations. He had a few and then slept like a baby infused with cough medicine.

"It could be car," his cleaning lady, Magda, a Bosnia survivor, suggested the next morning. "I very scare when car make bang." Magda cleaned up what was left of the glass ("Oh Mama in Paradise," she said, pulling a glinting sliver out of his mother's right eye glaring from the canvas, which was appropriate because that is where all of Magda's family now resided thanks to the sharpshooters in Sarajevo. His mother probably resided in hell. He would be willing to bet on that, no prayer in her lips when the plug was pulled.)

He agreed, the last thing he needed was to freak out his cleaning woman, who, because of language barriers, didn't realize other cleaners were getting minimum wage, plus carfare, plus lunch.

His dog, who normally thought the world was her big green latrine, refused to go outside, relieved herself in the shower. She also ran and hid under the bed every time the phone rang.

One of those calls was from me. I had bought a new dress and had hired a bartender and catering for two hundred for my launch party. He was publishing my book on erotic Inuit art, how to make love in a snowsuit, and my copy edit was overdue, about five years overdue.

"I can't talk; someone is trying to kill me, and my dog is pissing in the shower," he said, and hung up. Translation, the copy edit had met an obstruction similar to the one that made a necessity of daily enemas and prune juice. I decided to cancel the bartender and the catering and wear the lovely new dress to a family wedding.

Have you noticed the world is ass over teakettle? We have had four major seismic events in the Ring of

Fire over the past year; a hurricane has flattened New York and New Jersey; a bunch of billionaires have spent billions on an election that didn't return as much as a loaf of bread; and Barney's in New York is featuring an anorexic size zero, five-foot-eleven-inch Minnie Mouse in Jimmy Choo heels and a Vera Wang dress in their tweeners display.

So who cares if my book comes out? Well, me for one. I spent three freezing years living in igloos, researching sex in sealskins and polar bears with six legs.

Let me explain. I have in my small collection of aboriginal art a carving of a six-legged polar bear. The sculptor, grateful to a missionary for saving his soul and uniting him with his one true love in a Christian marriage, rewarded him with a sculpture of two mating bears. This makes sense. Were we not instructed by the gospels to go forth and multiply? However, the priest rejected the gift, praising the carver's skill but insisting he could not own a piece of pornographic art.

The carver, a practical man, took back the sculpture, shaved off the head and forelegs of the male bear, leaving a female with six legs, a startling likeness to the current Pope. Now doesn't that interesting artefact deserve the attention of the literate public?

Unlike my publisher, I do not have opiate dreams. Mine are of the pragmatic, straight-up archetypal variety. That is, when I am not in too deep a sleep to remember them. After the phone call, I closed my eyes and saw polar bears jumping from melting floe to floe, and come to think of it, wondered whence cometh that particular dream flow? My dictionary says it is from the Norwegians, who, after they die of cold are sent out to sea in burning boats. Perhaps someone will send my publisher a burning boat.

Whence the ice melt, and that is another story, perhaps enhanced by my desire for publication, the devil sacrament that uses up our sacred wealth of trees. Poor polar bears, balancing on shrinking floors, and not a rock in sight. So went my dream, and then I woke. Perhaps the bay window was penetrated by ice, and that would also fall into the deliberate column, deliberate but not so dangerous as a bullet.

I called him. "Maybe it was an icicle. Maybe the guy across the street was offended by your nakedness."

"Not a chance," he said, and went through the list of famous and beautiful men he had slept with, including the one who recently called a paparazzi a faggot, "I've never been rejected."

"How is the edit coming?" I asked. He made a dramatic and probably genuine exhalation of breath, and I saw my pages melting like ice floes, my book sinking into a cold artic sea.

Months passed. I heard that the editor had edited out the most alarming assassination options and accepted the randomness of fate. He had reopened his curtains, unlocked his front door and taken his disobedient dog for walks in the urban jungle half a world away from my vanishing tundra and the nuisance grounds that provided me with so much priceless material.

"Can't talk," he said before putting down the phone. "I've just been traumatized by a home invasion."

His Facebook account reported that a window washer had entered through the door on the second-floor balcony adjoining his bedroom. He had helped himself to the liquor cabinet, laid himself down on the bed and fallen asleep. The editor had arrived home on the late side, after an egregious literary event, a book launch (not mine, needless to say), and had fallen into bed without taking off his clothes. He thought the other warm body under the covers was his dog, and that was true, but his dog was just one of two warm bodies.

When he called 911, he reported a rape; but the story changed when the same officer who wanted to be a lawyer arrived with his partner, an attractive martial artist called Brenda, who was sleeping with him although both were married to other people. I mention this because it gives a certain frisson to the interview. In a subsequent call, my editor reported their conversation.

"You arrived home drunk."

"Yes."

"You took a cab, I assume."

"Uh..."

"I'll be checking."

"Am I the criminal here?"

"You might be. Did you walk the dog?"

"No."

"Wouldn't he have needed to go out?" The cop who wants to be a lawyer was once in the dog unit. He knows how much dogs need to be walked when their owners arrive home drunk, dew dripping off their nether lilies well after dew has fallen on the grass.

"I think I told you that my dog had been peeing in the shower."

"Yes, you did."

"I took off my shoes and fell into bed."

"Then what?"

"I had a dream."

"Yes?"

"I dreamed my dog was dying, and I had to give her mouth to mouth resuscitation."

"And you woke up kissing your dog on the mouth," Brenda guessed. She was learning vicariously.

"No, It wasn't my dog. It was the man who was in bed with my dog."

"And that man was...?"

"The window washer I hired on my way out the door yesterday morning."

"Then what?"

"Then he raped me."

"How did he do that?"

"The usual way."

"I'm sorry?"

"He penetrated me."

"I thought you were fully dressed."

"I must have undressed in my sleep. I'm a thrasher."

"You thrashed your clothes off, and then the window washer raped you."

"Yes."

At this point, Brenda and the cop who wanted to be a lawyer apparently lost their composure and had to retreat to their vehicle until they were able to handcuff their mirth.

I am a big admirer of John Irving who really gets the congruency of sex and death, baseballs in the forehead, penises bitten off during car fellatio. Perhaps my editor has bigger fish to fry, major popular novelist kinds of fish, and this is code for "Get lost. I have to see a man about a dog." Dogs, to me, à la Vermeer, conjure domestic fidelity, integrity, loyalty, all good things. I am confused. Perhaps my editor's dog is also confused. I doubt she's in on it, which constitutes animal cruelty, in my opinion, and my husband agrees with me.

My grandfather used to say that to me about his mysterious disappearances—I went to see a man about a dog. I didn't know whether he'd gone to the bathroom, to make a bet on dogs or horses or get in some putting practice. He certainly didn't mean, "I'm about to get into bed with a man and a dog."

I put my new dress in the closet, drank all the champagne (it was prosecco with the jar stopper lid, and we are going to use the bottles for vinegar, Christmas gifts. I doubt I will send one to my editor, but perhaps I should.). My husband, who shared the champagne and the loneliness of the endless nights I'd slept in the igloo a thousand miles away, suggested the shooter/window washer might be another writer.

We were now approaching the situation as a shaggy-dog story, vaudeville, a sutra with endless knots. We'd taken to role-playing, changing characters—sometimes I was the cop, sometimes the window washer. He was always the editor, the dog and/or the female cop (falsetto).

We made a joke out of eight years of my life.

I made one last call late in November, tongue ready to either give my editor a verbal lashing or lick the stamps on the box that held the last bottle of vinegar. He picked up the phone after nine rings and paused. If I weren't the caller and he the callee, I would have hung up. Those pauses never augur well. Most often it is someone in Asia or Nigeria who wants your money. Then I heard the dog barking. I made note of the timbre so I could encourage my husband to get perfect canine intonation during our next pantomime.

"I was out walking the dog," he said.

"That's good," I said. "So everything's back to normal again."

"N...n...n...o..." he answered. "Not at all. Someone shot at us in the park."

"Shot at? Are you dead then?" I like the idea of talking to zombies. It has the warm bullshit feel of a Caribbean breeze.

"Yes. I was wearing my cashmere coat, and it must have stopped the bullets."

"Ah, yes...." I wondered if that coat represented my share of his block grant, but pushed that thought back. I covered the receiver with my hand and told my husband to pick up in the kitchen, "....the Lamb of God. Did you feel it?"

"I felt a dull poke."

"A dull poke?" My mind went to the purple vibrator one of my husband's workmates used to beat up her unfaithful partner. But what I had meant by the question was, did he feel it in the religious sense, the Golden Fleece.

"Maybe it was nuns. Were you blocking the sacred path? Did someone poke you with a cane?" I have been to his house. It adjoins a convent, which is now a rest home for elderly nuns.

"That's ridiculous. The nuns adore us."

"Just a thought." His little bitch might have left a love offering on the convent lawn. "Did you phone the cops?"

"Of course, I went into the public toilet and called them on my cell."

"And?" I was thinking that was dumb. What if he'd been pursued in there, *if* being the big question?

"Nothing. I got the smart-ass cop who wants to be a lawyer."

"And what did he say?"

"Three strikes and you're out."

I could hear my husband snorting in the kitchen. He

couldn't help himself. I married him for his uncontrollable laughter.

"That sounds about right."

From now on, I'm going to write fairy tales.

THE LINEUP

Should we call it a cue, c-u-e, or queue with a q? It's a Chinese braid, a ladder to the sky, a hint of this lineup. Since we're all lined up for bread or butter or ladders to heaven, who cares how we spell it? Everyone's hungry for a turn at the tap or the tit. Everyone wants to get in or out: end-games, ultimate goals, desiderati. How do we convince them the cue is everything, the stick that swings and mails eight balls to happy holes and chalk into felt. Rrrriiiiippppp. Think tree of life, stick with branches. "It don't mean a thing if it ain't got that swing." Ask any golfer, or dancer or baseball player.

We're all in the game, and we all want to know how the play turns out, which portal to take: in or out, entrance or exit. But what happens now *in medias res,* before *deus ex machina?* Hurry up, please. We have a toothache. Our hair's too long. Our children are hungry. We need a Band-Aid, a fix. We have to pee.

But we are a rainbow, *la vie en rose,* red violet, indigo, hunter green, and the pot of gold is a box of chocolates, soft centers, artificial flavours, artificial colours, fake. Come on. Get in line. Now you will meet God and Beelzebub, the chorus of angels, whales connected by radar, the holy music, owls and ravens. Caaaawwww. Our cue.

I'm first. Thumbs up, middle finger, the body language meaning, I win, or fuck you, and in Cuba, first finger, not the Bernie wag but "*ultimo,*" me before you, but always first, even if you leave the line. *Ultimo*'s your body man, first through the door, and you follow, no matter what.

"*Ultimo,*" first on the bus, first in heaven or hell, first to jump off the end of the world, first to collect flannel bills stacked in deco banks with Tiffany lamps, where gangsters saved their money, first *helado,* first *pan.*

What did they do in the lineups at Dachau, where last was top of the pile, last puff of precious air. Not *ultimo.* What then? *Da capo,* from the top? Everybody died.

But this is theatre. We're lined up for the play inside, the play with a name and a cast of characters, a beginning, a middle and an end. Fringe=avante-garde, meaning "in front." Of course, there's a hierarchy in heaven, all the angels lined up according to rank, ready to jump off or into the thing we call life here on Earth, the most fragile lineup of all.

I'm first in line, *da capo,* born headfirst, the bomb, head ready to explode like a watermelon, the first bar in music, the *ultimo ultimo,* and number two is my spouse, who knows a banjo player who stood on his head for an hour when his parents sent him to a psychiatrist. Why?

Because he wanted to be an artist! Imagine that, when there's money in almost anything else they can think of: doctor, lawyer, captain of industry. *Artiste?*

Imagine their surprise when he pulled down his pants and put on a dress.

And number three, of course, because this is theatre and the whole world is the sidewalk outside a fringe venue, is Ladyboy, a shimmer of blue nails and elegant eyelashes, mascara mixed with tears running down his cheeks, followed by Girl With a Dangerous Weapon, her purse.

"Racist!" Girl yells, banging him hard. I won't admire Girl until I know the context because I once did the same thing to Mountie, who announced in the corner store, "Someone got hit by the train last night, but no problem. It was an Indian."

"It? Only a human life," I say, now as then, gripping my handbag hard, ready to strike.

"What did you do? What did you say?" I ask the ante-preultimate *ultimo.*

"I don't know," Ladyboy wails, and I wonder about moral equivalency, and who has the right.

"You guys stop this," I order.

Fat Woman with Fatter Shadow that stretches all the way down the block, who is next, says, "'Guys' is not PC. You might as well have said 'Bitches' or 'Niggers.'"

"Hey! All my relations, calm down."

And, as soon as my quick thinking *penultimo,* once called a Girl With a Weenie by a big bully, pulls out his comb and sings into it, his coloratura falsetto almost as back-archingly beautiful.

"Nice comb, Dude."

He responds by combing his beard.

Racism Girl huffs out most of her soul, at least twenty grams, and takes off, like a swinging door in a hurricane.

A mighty wind.

"I've got one drop," she spits. One drop of what, I wonder?

"So what *did* I say?" Ladyboy still doesn't know. None of us knows. We all shrug, and Ladyboy insists. "It's gay bashing."

Maybe it is. But we're all glad it's over. *For now.*

Ladyboy checks out the next person in line as Fat Woman with Fatter Shadow raises her pointing finger. Next Person is checking her program, She looks up, "Where am I?"

"Life," I say. And I mean it, wondering where this lineup really leads.

"What's the show called?" Next person checks her list.

"Life."

"Serious?"

"No, comedy."

Two more people have arrived. One wants to go to the front because she is deaf. "I can read faces, but not if I can't see them. I *need* the front row."

Penultimo aka Spouse aka Girl With a Weenie trades places, and Deaf Person begins a tirade about a show she says she couldn't hear, even though she perks right up when the Ice-cream Man drives by.

"She was completely inconsonant, ran all her words together, and her tap dance was terrible."

"I thought you said you were deaf?"

"It doesn't matter. I could tell she was speaking too quickly."

Oh, I didn't think so. I turn to the line and give my alternating "Hutch'kwa," Salish thanks and what-the fuck-gesture, hands up, palms out, and notice the slight fellow at the end of the line looks familiar.

"You look familiar," I say, and Slight Fellow begins to tap dance.

Deaf and, shall I venture against political correctness to say, Dumb Woman fails to return to her shell like a snail assaulted by salt and sallies forth, *ultimo* finger pointed right in Slight Fellow's face, to tell him what she thinks of his show. Her reasons are great. She couldn't hear. She hates tap dancing.

"Did you know that African slipper dancers adapted to tap when slave owners banned drumming between plantations? Tap dancing was Morse code, the only conversation between separated families. How does that make you feel?"

My face is in her face, and I know she can hear me. I know she can smell my breath. When I am mad, my breath smells like a maritime storm, fish stranded on the beach.

Ultimo starts to sing, "How does it feel?" and the line shrugs as Slender Fellow steps right out and taps on the sidewalk.

"He's telling you to lay off," Fat Woman with Fatter Shadow tells her.

"Back of the line," I say when she tries to edge herself back in. "No perks."

Dumb Woman does what she's told. Takes up the caboose position and pulls pen and paper out of her pocket. She uses Slight Fellow's back as her desk, and he lets her. Turn the other cheek, that guy said. Wow.

Girl comes out of the theatre, fully made-up, action doll ready for action, her purse in tow.

"Are you still here?"

"I will be, until I'm not."

"Admit you said it."

"Said what?"

"I said, 'Welcome to Whiteoria' and you said 'What?'"

"What?"

"Yeah, what?"

"Sorry."

"So you're apologizing?"

"No, I mean sorry as in, what did you say?"

"I said, 'WHITEORIA.'"

"I thought you meant Victoria."

"No I didn't. Look around you, everyone's white."

"Not me," Fat Lady says.

"Not me," Ultimo, unofficially Semitic, says.

"Not me," says New Guy, an Aboriginal who just came by with the drum from his show. "I just took heat from a critic who said my two-thousand-year-old choreography was amateur."

"The newspaper retired him, and not a moment too soon," Ultimo says, and the whole line except Dumb Woman, makes the Salish thank-you gesture.

"Hutch'kwa" in unison.

How does it feel, Critic Person, to be circling the drain surrounded by unsympathetic Indians? New Guy beats his drum harder.

"I'm done," Dumb Woman steps out of line to read her letter.

Dear aggrieved lineup,

I think I have been unfairly targeted. This is a free country and I expressed an opinion. I said Slender Person's show was a waste of an hour. An hour is precious to me. This lineup is my only chance to be heard. I am old and no one cares what I think. I am deaf and no one tries to communicate.

I'm not sexist, please understand. Life is a bitch and so am I. I need to know who is a girl and who is a boy.

"What the fuck does that have to do with it?" Ladyboy and Racism Girl shout in unison. Suddenly we're all on the same page. All except Dumb Woman.

"I found it confusing."

"Life is confusing," New Guy asserts.

And it dawns on me. The line isn't moving, and it isn't going to. I step ahead and try the door. Locked.

"We've been had, guys."

"How so?" New Guy asks.

"Why did you come here?"

"Someone gave me a comp."

"Me too," the line says in unison.

"Well the show is over unless you want to stand here until you freeze your asses off."

"We're it," says Ultimo who finishes my sentences and makes the coffee.

"Yes, how about a hand," I say, and we clap in unison.

"That's a good start," I say, "clapping together."

SHOCK THERAPY

My finger's in the socket," I yelped. It was 4 AM. He gave his pillow an extra squeeze and rolled over, but even though I'd sprained my neck bouncing off the ceiling, I was charged up, ready to jump into nautical twilight.

Splash!

This event came out of the blue. Ever since the election of the Bratman who spooned alternative truths to baskets of deplorables and evicted the black man from the White House, I have been waking up to the death of civilisation, mass Exodus, one refugee at a time: an intelligence operative, an artist, a singer, a comedian, a poet, a beautiful child, all of them rising, letting out air, the shhhhhit sound of Armageddon, deflating helium balloons, the laugh diaspora.

"Where the hell are they going?" I ask in the time between midnight and dawn.

"To the power source," my husband mumbles.

Is that it? I know the science. We're mostly water. Good conductors.

Weren't we all told not to fondle sockets and, "Don't

cross your eyes, they will stay that way." "Cross your legs, or boys will see," what? Pussy? Cunt? The unspeakable, until now, a different now, where Omega is Alpha, and cautionary stories have been taken over by spin.

While my mother's friends dispensed alternative parables to keep their kids in line, they took pills, Mother's little helpers, to stay thin and calm while their pinhole pupils raced around virtual clocks. While they jiggled their cellulite to death on Stauffer couches, their curious daughters hunted sockets, sometimes licking their fingers first.

Many of my mother's friends were hustled off to shock therapy when the inevitable happened: when their husbands fucked their secretaries despite their desperate efforts to stay young and viable, when they ran out of Kraft cheese and marshmallow recipes, when they ran out of children to poison with red dye number 4, when their daughters discovered the pleasant sexual nature of power surges.

It's all about electricity.

Despite my re-charge, I'm still in bed, scrolling through the news feed while He delivers many cups of coffee, so many my hands are shaking, or is it the stories about the child who was shot in the head and the child refugee in handcuffs; but then, hallelujah, a photo of snowdrops and one of a quetzal with tail feathers three times longer than the rooster's middle finger.

OK. That's breaking even. I can start my day.

Today there's a vigil for Muslims murdered at prayer:

fathers, a pharmacist, a beloved professor. I'm charged, tooling up for protest: one pink pussyhat, one shawl, instant hajib, one I AM MUSLIM sign and my safety pin that promises sanctuary.

Time to get up, wondering, is my dream a death wish? When children write stories that are intolerable but truthful, the last line always reads, "Then I woke up from my dream," as if death didn't happen. This is the real alternative truth. We don't want to know, but death happens. At four AM. It does.

Mothers say, "Use your words" to frustrated children, the ones who use sticks and stones to make a point, but not mine. Mine gave me a pencil and lined paper. Silence was golden. Then. Please, try not to win every argument. NO ONE WILL WANT TO MARRY YOU.

But not any more. I've been married several times, well, twice, but hyperbole is a poet's prerogative.

By the time my mother hit menopause, many of her friends had disappeared. Some of them joined cults, and some died of amphetamine overdose. Mothers' little helpers turned out to be their pallbearers. Some who remain are considering assisted death. The rest have dementia.

My mother says straight women are the problem, and up to a point, I agree, having watched too many of us morph into Barbies and rooster surrogates as the misogyny of the right and left drowned a relatively ethical woman in fake news.

We are self-cannibalising, a hen characteristic, and it is ugly to watch, especially the rooster surrogates, injecting themselves with Botox and fake tan, blonde variations on beef jerky wrapped in tinfoil, under orders to "dress like ladies."

So I join the sisters of the resistance who have crossed the bridge from dormancy during the years of affirmative action to real action. Again. I keep putting my finger in the socket. Welcome to the zombie jamboree. Soon you will be reading that I lit a fuse somewhere along the Mexican border.

But today is the day for prayer and meditation on the persecution of innocents, the horrible stutter of social repetition.

I am still crossing the bridge, pumping my charged fist in the air when I realise I have forgotten to do up my seatbelt. Not exactly forgotten. I couldn't turn and shoulder check with a stiff neck in restraint when I backed out of the driveway. That was deliberate. Then I did forget, because I got caught up in the pussy mantra (We will overcome!) and thoughts of the newly dead: my intelligence source, who recently corroborated the report about the Rooster's Russian connection, an artist of great energy whose power was short-circuited by deliberate indifference, the poet who wrote about a woman who decapitated her husband and poured his brain into a bowl of cereal.

So many stories about roosters and hens!

There's a little known fact about roosters. Most of them are terminated at birth. Shredded. Animal rights people are working on sexing eggs so their crowing is silenced before viability. Having witnessed the sociopathic behaviour of roosters, I like the shredding option, would like to see the Demented Rooster shredded in public, before the United Nations, which he is out to destroy with shock and awe tactics, diversion and simultaneous lightning strikes.

No one said roosters lack barnyard smarts. They put on quite a display with their feathers and spurs, their cock-a-doodle-dos.

But we are smarter. We are the daughters of Lysistrata, Salome and Queen Esther, "Off with his head," resonating in our genes. I should probably put my money on the Slovenian, who could be a true seraph, the agent of ultimate justice, her slutty photos and nudges and winks all code, "I'm with you." My hope is she's busy booby-trapping the golden tower, threading fuses through the elevators and tacky restaurants, sharpening her golden chopsticks from Mott 22 in anticipation of the moment she sticks one in his ear.

Poor King Swear, his Kingdom for a good otolaryngologist.

I am crossing the bridge, thinking these thoughts and neglecting to do up my seatbelt until lightning strikes, *Eureka! Buckle up! Get your finger out of the socket.*

He sees me do it. Probably thinks I saw him first, but no. I could run him over. He jumps in front of the car with his flat hand out. I think he's a distraught motorist.

"You could get yourself killed," I say, rolling the window halfway because he might be the angel of death

I missed this morning, or a highwayman.

"That's my line," he says, indicating my unengaged buckle.

This is when I see the discrete badge.

"I'm on my way to the vigil," I say. I am not trying to get out of a ticket. I just want him to understand. "I have a stiff neck. In the middle of the night, I put my fingers in an electrical socket." I trust him with this information, because I can't see him putting me into a padded cell, wearing the straightjacket you can bet I'd embroider with feminist slogans, bad optics for the cops.

There is something familiar, ah yes, my informant, the Balkan specialist. If I tell the cop that just before my friend passed he told me the dead man walking in Britain was a credible source. Would that information take him to the Cop Oscars, a promotion?

I am not thinking of this as a chess move, simply as reality television. This is the cop show finale, where I might get the rose.

I have hated cops for over a decade, ever since five giant babies in blue beat up a street person, then tasered him, while I, the only witness apart from a pot grower who was afraid to speak up, objected. Picture me, a middle-aged woman driving a Volkswagen pussy-car in glasses and granny shoes. Picture them, five armed toddlers with adrenalin grins, coming at me with threats, "Off with her head."

Picture me giving them the middle finger.

That was life changing. Trust me, I have been vicious:

refusing to buy cop raffle tickets, boycotting Cops for Cancer benefits, giving the resting bitch face to every schoolyard cop in the crosswalk, screaming at the black-child murdering cops on the news. Hating is hard work. I am tired of it.

This cop looks like my dead friend from MI6. He has kind eyes. He hands me a ticket, "Stop putting your finger in sockets." I feel a slight shock when his fingers touch mine, the Michelangelo effect.

"I'll be late for the vigil." I say, stunned. Is this my annunciation, my re-creation?

"Drive safe," he says. "I like your hat."

The vigil is over when I get there.

Am I supposed to go back to the bridge and give him my pussyhat? Would that be reparations/reconciliation? It's worth a shot.

But he's not there. Was he ever? Thinking I might be living inside a sitcom, I check my box: three walls, check; screen, check; sound, on.

I'm still plugged in. He's checked out, and I know I didn't imagine him because the ticket is written on real paper. I have a feeling we're going to meet again, maybe not at the The Supreme Court but possibly on some other golden path. Isn't that what we're supposed to believe?

DARLING BOY

I didn't feel a thing. Hair doesn't have feelings. Not even red hair. Not even when I'm stoned. Especially when I'm stoned; and that's an important detail because the cop who went to the Cop Oscars for arresting that famous bank robber dragged me all the way up the cliff from Mile Zero by my ponytail the night me and my buddies got busted for hanging at the beach.

I'm a ginger, and that means hard to stone, hard to put out for surgery, but easy to piss off.

But I'm not. Pissed at Daisy. Fair is fair. I have all the advantages. I can remember the magic numbers to get in and out. I get to choose the books we read and the food that I eat. Daisy just got it in her head she wanted some kind of keepsake, snuggled up close as if to see the pictures in the book about Wounded Knee, and gotcha, I was missing some ginger and she was dancing inside a circle of Dementia Girls whooping like Sitting Bull's warriors. Lucky I was wearing my magic shirt full of roach holes that never burned me. Who knows, she might've thought of hacking off some skin.

"Where'd you get these?" I put down our book, got up,

disarmed her gently, and brought her back to her chair. Daisy doesn't need scissors. People come in to fix her hair and her nails. The nurses chop up her food. She put her handful of my crowning glory in her pocket with a smirk I would never call a smile. It was pure naughty.

"No more ghost stories," I warned her. "They give you bad ideas."

"You mad at me?" She grabbed my hand and kissed the fish webbing between my fingers. Ginger on speed, they said before I quit swimming. How many husbands did she waste? Daisy can charm the seeds out of a nickel bag.

"I'm mad about you," she said, half-singing, so I knew it was an old tune. Daisy is a human jukebox. I wish I had half that number of songs in my head.

Matt the physio says we're an item. That's a relief to him because all the other ladies stalk him. It started when he asked the Dees to make like they're windshield wipers and she couldn't get her arms going in opposite directions.

"Unison's good," I said, and we did it together. That got her laughing.

"She never laughs," Matt said, and that was how I got off janitor duty and became her special reader, even after my hundred hours were up. We have a connection. She calls me Darling Boy because she can't remember my name. That's OK by me. When you're a ginger with your name on the cop blotter, anonymity is a true endorphin hit.

Daisy does remember some things. Unison got her going. Her brain is wired for opera. A nurse gave her earphones so she could listen in private; but she sings along, and we all try to get through it without wetting ourselves, especially when she dances. She's dem bones dancing.

I like reggae myself. Daisy made a face when I downloaded a bunch of tunes, but she did get up and shake her moneymaker, or the handful of skin that's left of it. Matt laughed his face off.

"You got her number all right."

"She's got mine too." I make like I'm dialling up the lonely muscle on the left side of my ribcage. Daisy is cool with me, and she never tells me to do my homework, go to school, cut my hair or quit smoking ganja. That would be my business. I've taken charge of my life, and I have a new family, all friends, and no blood relations.

In a way, it was her idea to get me working with the dementia team. One morning when I was still chipping off my hours with a broom, I found her redecorating the dayroom, moving the chairs around. You've got to know, some of those chairs, especially the La-Z-Boys, are heavy, and she's a small lady. Just to give you a picture, I'll tell you she's about a handspan over five feet tall, and she eats as much as an ant can carry in one load. Daisy wears yellow, and she smells like dandelions. Even when she's just had her hair done, she wears a sunhat with fake flowers stuck in the band.

"Awesome, you're a monster," I said, watching her

motorize chairs, wondering what she was on. “What’s up?”

“We need a meeting.” Daisy wasn’t even puffed out. This is the lady who calls her visits to the washroom “hikes.”

“What about?”

“You know,” she said, one of her two standard answers. One is “You know,” and the other is “Sometimes yes, and sometimes no.” Either way she avoids making mistakes. I think she is way more with it than she gets credit for. I should have answered like that at school. They might’ve thought I was Einstein throwing the questions back at them.

“No, I don’t.”

She let go of the chair she was scraping across the linoleum (“It’s got to be linoleum because some of the girls pee themselves,” she’d confided) and whispers, “We’re all prisoners here. They won’t let us back into Canada. It isn’t fair. We’re Canadians.”

“You’re right,” I said. “It isn’t.”

“So we’re going to have a revolution,” she announced, Daisy proud of Daisy for dialling the right word that time.

“Oh.” That’s what I got for reading her stories about Che, Louis Riel and Sitting Bull. Back in Canada, I’m willing to bet she voted Conservative but in Deeland, Daisy’s gone rogue. I wondered if I should sneak in a joint. It might help with her constipation.

“You have to help.”

“What am I going to do?” At this point in my life, I feel I’ve got as much potential as ice cubes in hell.

"You're going to make a speech."

"A speech? Me? What about?"

"You're going to tell them."

"Tell them what?"

"To let us out and in."

"Where?"

"Canada. We want in. It's our right."

"You've got to give me some time."

I noticed the Dees had put away their blank expressions, which only happens when little kids and dogs come into the ward. They were smiling and winking at me. Daisy really had them worked up, which was neat, but it totally maxed my stress level. This could land me in jail, which I barely avoided last time I stuck my red head up. Jail scares the crap out of me. I've heard ginger boys get the eggbeater where the sun doesn't shine if they step out of line; and who decides where the line is anyway?

"OK. I'll make a speech tomorrow." And maybe I'll never come back, I thought.

Soon as I got out of there, I lit up a doobie and walked around the hospital 'hood. It was spring and colour saturated, like being in a Johnny Depp movie. (They don't call Victoria the Garden City for nothing.) Daisy loves her garden walks. Isn't that Canada enough for one old lady?

The trippy gardens handed me a plan. The deck off the dayroom is big enough to have a name, and there was nothing growing in the planters, somebody's great idea gone to waste. I knew what to do.

Daisy hadn't forgotten. Soon as I walked in with my big garbage bag, she and her ladies crowded around me like hens at feeding time (I used to look after the chickens at our farm). I have to admit the dementia ladies *smell* like a henhouse.

"Well?" she asked, white knuckles gripping her hipbones.

"OK," I said. "Back off, ladies. Follow me. We're going to Canada." I led them to the door.

"Canada?" she said when they were all outside on the deck.

"Yes. Inside is purgatory." (I know that word from my brief incarceration at Sunday School). "Outside is Canada." I let them peek in my bag. "I have some plant donations."

From that moment, everything changed. We planted and weeded. The Dees, God's gaga gardeners, got high on flowers. When the days got shorter, we had a great Indian summer and the petunias, marguerites, geraniums and pansies I got with the five-finger discount sailed into fall with all their flags flying.

Most days, the ladies stayed outside in Canada and fussed over their plants. When it rained, Daisy cranked up her headset and danced in the dayroom, and they boogied with her, waving their watering cans. Could've been a zombie jamboree.

"You believe in zombies?" I asked Matt.

"I believe everything I see, brother."

"I think there is life after death."

"You might be right."

"Maybe reincarnation. My mother tells me I'm going to come back as a cockroach."

"Could be worse." He moved off with his smooth smile and a basket of squeezie balls for arthritis exercises, leaving me with my cranky criminal, wondering what worse might be.

"You shouldn't have cut my hair, Daisy. It's a boundary violation. I have an OC problem: No wrinkles in my bed and every hair in place." I patted my head to make the point.

She wasn't listening, and her eyes were one hundred percent pupil, black holes of forgetfulness you wouldn't want to fall into. If I didn't know better, I'd say she'd had a bad dose. Just when I peered into the void, she reached right in my pocket and clawed back the scissors. Then she took off for Canada.

I got up real slow. I was afraid to run after her in case she tripped and fell on the blades. Freaky samurai. Read the headline, "Ginger stalks sweet old lady with scissors."

While I was walking on eggs, the Dees lined up at the window. It was lunchtime, but they were more interested in watching Daisy snip. Who cared if the soup got cold? By the time I tiptoed close enough to hear what she was saying, she'd ripped off half the petals, "He loves me/He loves me not."

"Give me the scissors, please." I put my hand out.

"He loves me not." She shouted, "Off with their heads," and I didn't know what to do. Daisy was fully armed, and I was scared to death she was going to hurt herself. Snip. Snip. Petals fell like infantry.

At the picture windows, the Dees clapped and cheered, their mouths and eyes as blank and psycho as the characters in Japanese comics. This gave her more energy. She was a human smart bomb, taking everything down.

"Please."

"Party's over," Matt said. He came up so quietly behind her, his white hospital shoes could've been moccasins.

"You're damn right." Daisy turned, handed over her weapon of mass destruction and announced, "Time for a time-out."

Matt put her hand in the crook of his elbow and guided her down the hall, singing, "Daisy, Daisy, Give me your answer do," but she wasn't having any of it. She stuck out her foot and delivered all two hundred pounds of Matt meat straight to the floor. He didn't see it coming. The Dees, afraid of reprisals, I guess, an extra dose of the prune goo, poo on a spoon, after lunch, slunk toward the dining room, and I stayed put.

"Give her time," Matt said when he came back, limping slightly but looking brave. "They're serving shrimp salad sandwiches with the soup. She loves shrimp day."

I knew what he meant. Like a dog, Daisy can smell chocolate in my pocket.

"OK. I'll give it a couple of days." It was time for me to shuffle off to the candy store. Daisy'd hid a twenty in my book before she cut me. The Dees aren't supposed to give us tips, but it wasn't for me, not all of it. She rewards me for bringing in contraband. Daisy has a sweet tooth, but she isn't allowed candy because of the diabetes. Heck, she's ninety. Why not die happy with a wad of toffee stuck to your false teeth?

Reprisal time, I got high on her dime and ate most of the candy myself, and now, after waiting three days, I'm dropping in with a bag of gummy bears and a new library book, *The Edge of Physics,* a journey to Earth's extremes to unlock the secrets of the universe. That should challenge both of us. I can't even pronounce the writer's last name.

Zippety doo dah, it's an awesome morning. When I punch in my numbers and tiptoe into the dayroom (I was going to come up behind her and put my hands over her eyes), Daisy's nowhere to be seen. I look out the window at Canada, and she isn't there either. There are no new faces on the flowers. It looks like the grim reaper's been out there.

"Where's Daisy?" I ask, but the Dementia Ladies give me their who-are-you looks. I undertake a search.

She's in her room. Matt is sitting beside her bed, one of her manicured hands in his brown one, the other gripping the keepsake she took without permission.

"It's closing time," he says. "Daisy's decided." He says this like she still gets to and lets me take it all in for a minute: the stuffed animals, the dead violets, the black-and-white photos on her table and Our Lady of the

Deadheads herself lying there quiet and pale.

"She got into bed after you left the other day, and she's refusing to eat or drink. Not your fault. This is what they do when they're done."

Then we're quiet. I hear rubber soles in the hall and shallow breathing. The nurses come by and take her pulse. One of them shows me the blood pooling at her knees, and I notice her toenails are painted bright pink. Day turns into night. After forever, I hear Daisy go "Oh!" letting go of a surprised little puff of air, and Matt stands up.

"Time's up," he says, stretching, watching with me as her fingers stiffen around the curl she stole.

He gives me a big man hug and says, "Her son was a redhead, Darling Boy."

DEADHEAD: WHAT GOES AROUND

She's heavy because she's not helping, her eyes focused beyond the garden, the blossoming Japanese cherries, the camellias and snowdrops poking their heads up, dear companions, tired old bulbs, those resilient ladies past dissembling, Botox and dye, which she would notice if she were paying attention.

"Way past her stale date," her older one, twin born first, turns her face, but not enough, and mutters because she is deaf, but not so deaf she can't read lips.

"Lips" is a trigger. She experiences a tremour in the earthquake zone.

It's her birthday, and she can safely predict they have brought the usual beautifully wrapped gifts, probably scarves, socks or gloves, but what she really wants is to get laid, probably not by their angel-faced gaily attentive Hispanic waiter, nor any of her co-resident foggy old men with their John Henrys sauntering out of the nether plackets in their pajamas, sometimes shooting to attention when a nurse bends over, when they catch their scent, and certainly not by a banana. Do not, daughters of Satan, order me a banana split and giggle. Of course, they won't; this is a proper restaurant.

She's looking past the grunting team lifting her out of her wheelchair and onto her favourite bench on the terrace facing the sea, sailboats, the San Juan Islands, where her grandmother's rum-running coolies, clandestine pirates, delivered opium then whiskey during the Prohibition.

It's too predictable. They *will* order for her: soup, crab bisque, easy to swallow, and crème caramel. She does not want crème caramel. Yes, it has been her favourite; the egg is a perfect shape, it's function oval, made for simple delivery, so handy the way the cloaca turns inside out and keeps it clean. Beautiful. She admires hens for everything but their congress with roosters. That is humiliating, especially now that a rooster has taken over the free world.

One interesting fact that she knows and her daughters might not is that roosters do not have penises. Just little holes. They grab, line up the holes and squirt. No please, no thank you, no handshake.

She won't touch her dessert today, and her daughters will fuss. They will fill the spoon and poke it in her mouth; and she will keep her mouth shut. Tight. She keeps up her Kegel exercises, both ends, both velvet creases sharp.

The crab bisque she will eat. And when she lifts the shaking spoon to her lips, they will watch. They will give one another the look, almost the eye roll they perfected as teenagers. Look what's happening. We'll have to send that lovely dress to the dry cleaners....again. Sigh.

The girls take all her laundry home. There's pilfering at the home, and voilà, one wash and a Simon Chang turns into MADE IN TAIWAN. The dementia club laundry has ruined her 800 thread count Egyptian sheets and a number of pleated scarves. DO NOT LAUNDER ANYTHING, one daughter left the note on her closet door after taking down a favourite drawing of Besus, the crucified Easter rabbit, by her great-grand-niece, replacing it with the laundry notice and DRESS (not please, just "Dress, capitol D") MOTHER IN THE CLOTHES WE LEAVE ON THE HANGER. Nothing else. Every day is perfectly coordinated: slacks, blouse, sweater and scarf, all from a soft garden palette, dusty rose with the palest greens, olive and aubergine, blue and gold. God help her mix-and-match nurse's aide, a Filipina putting several children through med school.

She is their doll. They dress her up, give her manicures, feed her and then abandon her to medicated sleep. It is lovely when they tiptoe away. She doesn't tell them about her dreams, about the delicate arousals, men she has known and imagined, suppressed moans. That is what she keeps for herself. Private. None of their damn business.

They order martinis for themselves. Doubles, three olives. The olives are their food. "We would like a cup of the crab bisque and a custard for dessert," her eldest daughter by twenty-three minutes tells the waiter, her aha moment. “We.” They are so predictable. The waiter winks at her, and she understands that he gets it. He too may be in some sort of prison. What for, maybe the crime of being gay or not getting the part in the television series, or not being helped through school by a bed-making, diaper-changing mother?

She likes him. He is attractive in a millennial metrosexual biracial way, helpful with a touch of irony, an alluring accent and no sycophancy. She will slip him a bill when they look away, if they do look away. Her girls have the focus and ferocity of eagles circling fields teeming with mice. They dislike it when she rewards people for kindness, staff and street people who wish her a good day, a little flirtation, her pleasure. She has a stack of twenties stashed in her bra.

What she sees in the foreground now is something like that, the hotel garden, circles of Hell on Earth, eggs, yes, half-naked women by the glass-covered pool, tempting men: pool cleaners, dreamers, serpents, garden snakes and toads, the old story, leering oligarchs, their chest hair glittering with gold man-chains.

Above and beyond is the beckoning tunnel, clouds, bright light, that blazing star, Lucifer, and seagulls singing, ocean filling up with human abuse, the bodies of discarded coolies and plastic bags. She lowers her glasses for a moment, watches the hard edges smooth out, cloud on cloud, light on light, a perfect platform for a diabolical angel, the one who might fuck her on the way out, or in.

"The pool is full of piss," she says, settled now, oily old man pee. "They never admit it. Everyone does it." Her daughters smirk. They know about the diapers, of course they do, the bitches. They have no idea how hard she works to avoid accidents, the Kegels, morning, afternoon and night.

She loves these bitches. Or she did. Once they were babies, adorable sausages with pinched wrists and dimpled elbows, crushable fairies in party dresses with layers and layers of ruffles, but that is over. Now she's working through the third stage of grief, letting them go. Phase one she almost missed, making excuses for the lapses in respect, the missed appointments punctuated by regular appeals for financial assistance, the houses, the holidays, the divorces. How long did it take to see the insides of those houses, always under renovation, not appropriate for entertaining, not even a cup of tea?

Stage two was the worst, giving up her house, her car, her financial freedom, all because she occasionally forgot to turn off a tap or the stove. Everyone makes mistakes now and then. What is a mistake or two compared to a life sentence? Let the punishment fit the crime. She will never adjust to the loss of freedom, her studio, the smell of paint, and incarceration in the pink prison, smooth food, pureed vegetables, drinks with a straw and sandwiches with the crust cut off. The crust is the best part, for God's sake. It makes your hair curl.

"Your glasses, Mum," Number Two tries to rescue them and almost puts her finger in her eye.

"I'm having an impressionist moment," she says, not angrily but firm enough. She likes the colours running together, her theory of the universe, everything indivisible, one. Three cheers for myopia.

"No walls," Number One says, agreeably. They agree, in principle. One is a follower of the Dalai Lama. Two is more practical, more attached to the phenomenal world by virtue of coming into it almost a half hour later, and always worried she has missed something.

The drinks have come: two martinis with three olives and a glass of water floating a forlorn lemon slice. No straw though. It's her birthday.

"I would like a martini too."

"Oh Mum," Two says, "Remember the last time?"

"Of course not. I have pre-dementia. Remember? You made it up to get power of attorney." In fact, she is an attorney. One is a photographer, and that should be common ground, but obviously isn't. Her statement, "I'm not an artist. It's just a living," the stake in her heart.

"Last time, Mum, you asked the waiter if he was going to serve sex on a platter."

"Did I? How adorable. Was he pleased?"

"No, he was amused, but definitely not into it. Also you yelled. The whole restaurant stopped dead."

"Not the whole restaurant, surely? We always sit on the terrace. That is only PART of the restaurant."

"The whole terrace."

"How embarrassing for you."

"Well, you are not getting one this time." She closes her fists with the thumb sticking up and holds them close to her side. That began when she was two. There is a certain advantage to being an elder. Elders remember everything from before, until they don't. And then it hardly matters.

"Would you like your gifts before or after you eat?" One lurches after a distraction.

"After." She reminds herself "gift" means poison in German.

She would like to take out her hearing aids and just watch the two of them opening and closing their mouths, obsessively checking their phones.

"It's like watching fish in a tank," she says.

"What?" Unison.

"Deafness," she says. "It's like being in space or under the sea." She is, if anything, faster than they are, a real improviser. Their mouths hang open. She could swim right into them.

"Here's your soup, Mum. Two more martinis please."

"Three."

"Two."

Their waiter falters and smiles. "Three," he says, exploding the adorable folds in his cheeks where the fairies kissed him.

"You are an angel."

"That is my name."

Yes, she can read the embroidery on his shirt, but he says, "On Hell," and that pleases her. That fits the theme of her day.

"I like your dimples, On Hell," she says as he walks away in the shoes of the fisherman.

"What's *my* name," Two asks, hungrily, she thinks.

"Does it matter?"

"She's losing it." One agrees.

"It's my birthday," and, she taps one of the four hands lunging at her spoon, "I will feed myself."

The soup is very good, tender scallops and baby clams in a creamed potato and oyster base. Yum! The focaccia is good too, just the right amount of rosemary, not overwhelming. Nothing is overwhelming.

"Dessert is on the house for the birthday senorita," On Hell, her Hispanic prospect, says, serving their drinks. Hers has seven olives, one she assumes for each angel of the apocalypse, and is in a bigger glass. Good boy. She could take a bath in that glass.

"I don't want dessert," she says, "unless you have a bag of Cheetos and a match."

"Been there, done that," he says in his charming accent, exposing his dimples again. "Pow!" Maybe that is the real reason why he left home and the mother who can't help him become a neurosurgeon, a trail of arson, blowing up overprivileged daughters. She finds that possibility strangely erotic.

And they laugh. Or he does. And she does, confirming On Hell is her angel of light.

Daughter One furiously inhales her martini and begins to choke.

On Hell moves to save her with the Heimlich, a chance to practice.

"Leave her," she snaps, watching One's face turn blue and then Two, at long last, thumping her back until she spits up the olive.

"You two should be in a rest home. Where are my presents before you are too senile to remember where you put them?"

"Mum, you are supposed to be happy. It's your birthday."

"I *am* happy."

"What's with the Cheetos?" Two asks, hauling something out of her purse.

"It's political," she answers." Cheetos are code for anarchy. They're made of petroleum, and they blow up."

"So you want to blow us up?"

"Not really. I just like to start fires."

"As in unfriending every Trump supporter on Facebook, even the ones you've known since the Stone Age?"

"And the Bernies. Alt Right, Alt Left, no difference. It's all about oil, but somehow it boiled down to misogyny."

"So what does that have to do with us, right here, right now?"

"I am not the enemy. You are supposed to be my allies."

"Who said we weren't?" Two's eyes the colour of sage at sunrise fill with tears. Two is the daughter of what used to be called miscegenation, a sensational mix of Northern European and East African. One is the spawn of an Irish poet. It took her no time at all to figure that out. Although born twenty-three minutes apart, they were conceived on separate occasions. Maybe today she will tell them exactly how it happened and dispel their misguided belief that they were, contrary to her assertions, adopted separately.

"Well, here we are, Mum, treating you on your special day and you are not behaving."

"What is treating? Is treating paying for an opportunity to be condescending, ageist?"

"You're just upset because you're a year older."

Not at all. She embraces her age, as clearly they don't. They are clearly terrified of her liver spots and wrinkles, her buckled knees and crumbling hips. She looks from background to foreground and sees the cracks they fill in with potions and treatments. Her eyes fill up. Poor things. Their coddled generation keeps on believing in its own immortality while their own children plan their ultimate catch and no release.

Two tosses her package. "Here, I brought you something to cheer you up."

It lands in her lap, and she carefully removes the ribbon. Damn her arthritis. The bride-coloured pink-and-ivory bow is a bugger, but she's damned if she'll let on, just pretends she's building suspense. Then comes the tissue, layers of cream and pink petals.

"What is it?" The thing is green with glittering scales. "Is it a pickle, no, a flashlight?" She could use a flashlight for her late-night visits to the toilet.

"Warm, but no cigar."

"Is it an e cigar then, a big doobie?

"Funny you should ask."

"Push the button, Mum." One shows her where.

"Oh," she says, "it's an electric pickle."

"Yes," her girls sing in unison.

"I looked for yellow because you taught us how to..."

"Put a condom on a banana," she finishes.

"Yes, but I could only find a pickle."

"Because I told you that you'd be in a pickle if the condom failed."

"Right."

Things have taken a turn for the better. While her daughters drain their glasses, she opens her armadillo roadkill purse and pops it in. It just fits, *like a hand in a glove,* her biology teacher told the class when he was explaining human reproduction.

"To me," she says, and tosses her drink back.

"And these," One says, handing her two smaller packages, one is squishy and one not. "Guess."

"This one is for the pickle." She gives it a squeeze.

"Yes."

"And the other is a small cigar."

"Uh huh."

"Should we light it up?"

"You mean here," more unison.

"Why not? I'm heading for my holy bridegroom, best sex ever. Who would suspect?"

"The smell, Mum."

"We're outside, semi-outside. It could be skunk

cabbage. She unwraps the joint and holds it between her fingers, like a real cigarette.

On Hell is there before she can say, Welcome daughters of wormwood. Let the holy river explode, and he has a lighter.

"Allow me."

She leans into him, what was your name again, looks up at the sky, inhales deeply, and the golden tunnel convulses, her heart shuddering as the pastel light contracts. Blink, the aperture closes.

The daughters react in treble unison, a scream, the high note filling her portal, the unbirth canal one step closer to their own. Her children could be Queens of the Night as the afternoon goes dark. They stand and reach for her as she falls, but the waiter, the one called Angel, puts his hands out to stop them, then lifts her up in his arms.

"Make a wish," he says.

BLINK

I try not to blink. If I close my eyes, he will disappear and there are so many unanswered questions. Is that why we grieve? My father's eyes are open, but he's looking somewhere else, and that may be the answer I'm seeking, a matter of technique rather than distance. I remember the advice he brought from a great ballerina.

"Keep your eye on the place you want to end up, and you will arrive there."

Alternately dozing and pacing, I don't entirely agree. Life and art are not always identical. I took that advice to the turning point in my life, the night my best friend drowned in an icy river.

It's like the dumb show in prison when loved ones are separated by glass. I willed him to keep looking at me as I swam toward him, my arms numb with cold; but he quit. One moment his eyes were alive, and the next, nothing.

Before the drowning, I was most terrified of fire. In my dreams, I fell into cracks in the Earth, but my father said, "It's just other worlds down there," and he made up beautiful stories in that charmed interval between relaxation and insobriety.

Fire took my Wettums doll after a leak in her pipes made her insides rot. The letter from the doll hospital said she had a remarkable death. My dad told me about Vikings and the cautionary tale about Hindu suttee, widows burned with their husbands beside holy rivers.

"Not to worry, I've been there. Some day the Earth will move for you and you will like it."

In the beginning, I was his paper doll. He put on our favourite record and rode me to bed on his slippers, then disappeared into the dark. I fought sleep, but sleep grabbed me and threw me into the fire in Middle Earth.

My mother got to be God. One night, she burned all my worn-out dolls in the garden. The souls of the dead fell through holes that went all the way to China, the playground of lost toys.

For a while, I slept with my cap gun, fighting fire with fire. When he realised I was just starting new ones, my father gave me my favourite toy, a music box with a ballerina on top. "She's made of china," he said. "She's fragile but strong, just like you."

He placed her on my bedside table, turned on the lamp, wound her key, and together we watched her shadow dance on the wall. I wondered what could be on the other side, where discarded dance partners waited another turn. My ballerina, pirouetting *en pointe* to the tune of Tchaikovsky's "Rose Adagio" from *Swan Lake*, reached out. I don't recall my father leaving. That was invisible.

"Turn off the fucking news," my mother says in one of Dad's final moments. She can't stand to watch. Because my father drools and drops Kleenex like confetti on the carpeted floor of his tenth-floor apartment at Sunset Lodge, the screen is covered with spit. Why rest homes have carpets is a mystery. Perhaps they're breeding germs for the war against Hong Kong emigration and the mega houses my father called a stucco rash on Shaughnessy Heights.

It's after six. I turn down the sound, but leave the picture. Pamela the news anchor keeps speaking, moving her mouth in prime time/mime time, opening and closing the final curtain. Will my father be taking a bow with his ballerina or crawling past Pamela's luxuriant lips, red satin sheets, into his encore performance, or non-performance because we all know what alcohol does to libido?

We are all waiting for the adagio movement, my mother, my father and I. Soon we get to find out who is the angel of death and who swallows first.

My father is in love with Pamela on Channel 8 and Margot, *prima ballerina assoluto,* one vicarious and one unquestionably ephemeral dream girl, and that is the family blend, the game of who's who that rules our *ménage de trop.* Now, the news anchor is a dyed blonde, but years ago she began as the six o'clock raven-haired shape-changer.

He's no longer waiting for the new wife to come and give what she promised when they got married without inviting family to the ceremony. She has possession of the new house and the new car, and he's in the rest home, still anticipating the first conjugal visit, or any visit at all for that matter.

My sobered-up dad looks good in God's waiting room; skin as smooth as A Baby's Bottom, his favourite brand of pipe tobacco, eyes wide open, blue circles in saucers of milk, his mouth the surprised O, the final portal, last round door. The morphine is working.

My mother, flipping through the latest *Vanity Fair*, chewing gum, has less hair, more spunk. She is butch, her present incarnation. She came for her karma, and to protect his assets from the second wife should she arrive in time to snatch Dad's precious things (first editions) and the stack of hundreds he keeps in his bedside drawer.

He is not supposed to tip the staff, but he does, generously, "Can't take it with me." He certainly doesn't want too much left over for the extortionist wife. Tips or no tips, the nurses love him. He is handsome, Cary Grant handsome, with a full head of distinguished silver hair, a manly cleft in his chin and lots and lots of hundreds.

He knew Cary. The nurses love Dad's celebrity stories and admire him for his books and the framed photographs of his famous friends: Cary, Zsa Zsa, President Ford, the Mills Brothers, Errol and Margot.

In Margot's photo, she is dancing the "Rose Adagio," the song in my music box. It is signed, *"je t'adore."*

My mother has exactly the same picture with exactly the same dedication hidden under her bed where her hideous Peterbald cats wait to pounce and shred my ankles. My photo says, "Keep working at the *barre*." She knew the most I would get out of ballet would be better posture. I am much too tall for the chorus, and not everyone gets to be a soloist.

I am the daughter of soloists, and it is not a position I aspire to.

I brought my knitting and a book, but I can't focus. My father is doing that for all of us, his blues fixed on the near distance, possibly looking for the news anchor to reach out of the television or for the seagull that visits his balcony to take him for a spin. "My last friend," my father said, defying the house rules against feeding birds that defecate on the building.

He might be giving up the notion of romance in this world as he peers into the next.

My mother told me she had a dream in which Margot Fonteyn spun around her bed. "I heard wood. I thought it was woodpeckers." That was when I found out she too had a passion for ballet.

"Does she have a wooden leg?" I asked. I was not yet *en pointe* and had no idea how toe shoes are constructed. We knew a war amputee who hid chocolate in his leg. "No," she said.

"No," she says now to my brother who is holding a pillow over my father's face. She sees him too. He is the merciful one in spite of being called *ballet boy* by my father. He loves opera, and now I suppose he's a Valkyrie sent to collect the dead.

"That was then," our father has apologized, *then* being the period of grieving for courageous friends who died in the war that lasted to the point of indulgence.

The ballerina on my music box had china legs and a china body, and her tutu was layers of the palest rose. She had perfect *porte de bras* and never wavered, just turned round and round on one toe, one hand reaching out to her invisible suitors.

I was ten years old, not quite wise to the connection between the Earth moving and my lady's pirouettes. "This dance defines a great ballerina."

They called Margot Peggy. Her real name was Peggy Hookham, not a good name for a ballerina when all the others were Russian and French.

"Hooker," my mother said, derisively.

Nevertheless, she took me to see Margot and Soames, Margot and Nureyev. "They are lovers," she said, fixing her opera glasses on whichever beautiful man bottom, "You can tell." That made sense to me. Ballet is romance. Romance is boys and girls, or so I thought then. Nevertheless she went to London to stay with Margot, information she has only shared today.

My father must have been angry with my mother for taking her turn.

"Why not?" she said. "I am entitled to know what it's like."

The ballerina had many dance partners, Soames,

Nureyev, my parents, all of them stepping into the music and spinning until they vanished like the tigers in *Little Black Sambo.*

She blinked and she disappeared.

My parents argued. They used words like "obsession" and "adultery." My father said "sick," and later I realised he was being territorial. That night I over-wound my music box and my ballerina refused to dance, so I punished her by putting her under my bed.

When I came home from school the next day, she was gone.

"Margot is dead," my father said. My ballerina had danced into a crack in the floor, taking Margot with her. I'd killed both of them. But still I waited. Miracles happen. Lost things come home like dogs that travel thousands of miles.

I stopped dancing, and my great time of reading began. I read every book in my father's library under the covers, ruining my eyes. My parents separated.

After the longest time, my brother puts down the pillow. My mother rolls her eyes and jingles the keys in her pockets. I wonder if some of them are my father's keys. My high-school biology teacher told us animals mated successfully because their sexual parts fit like keys in locks. I close my eyes and imagine how my father might have wound her up, making my mother dance.

The six o'clock news has ended. Pamela signs off. Do I see a light go out in my father's eyes? Has he missed his chance to hitch a ride to the stars? I recently watched a child who wanted to hug Barney attempt to crawl inside the screen of a big TV at Costco. It broke my heart.

My mother, like a magician's sleeves and Lady Murasaki's, is full of surprises. She pulls something wrapped in a scarf out of the backpack filled with provisions for my father's farewell party—toothbrush, apple, granola bars, Kleenex—unties it and sets my music box on the bedside table.

Everyone in the room knows what it is.

"You had that thing all along?" I am incredulous. "I can't believe it."

"I never liked girls, except for sex," I once heard her confide on the phone from my hiding place in the closet with louvered doors. I already knew that. Until my brother arrived, she'd dressed me as a boy. Then I got my first leotard.

I needed to be in a love story, and ballet is all love stories.

"What is love?" Prince Charles famously asked on television the day of his engagement, because he knew his mistress was watching. They are all the same. My grandmother danced with the last Prince of Wales and so did several of her friends, one of whom claims he fathered her child.

Some say dance is foreplay. I thought it was love.

It is growing dark. I try not to blink in the moonlight that filters through the blinds. My mother is dozing. She will wake up with pleather creases in her cheek. "Braille farewell," I will say. It sounds like a tune for bagpipes, a Highland fling.

I turn on the bedside lamp when a nurse comes to check my father's pulse and his blood pressure. "It won't be long," she says. He's showing all the signs of approaching death. I am surprised by how young his legs look. It is as if he is moving backwards, back to the time when he used to ask me, who is the handsomest dad in the world?" and I stepped on his feet for a waltz while he headed for the door. "See you later, Alligator."

The sound of the winding key is a comfort in a room full of snores, my mother asleep and my father saving his breath. My ballerina stands on her little rose box, eyes on the prize, fixed on the spot where she'll end up, no matter how dizzy. That spot is the dark corridors in my father's eyes. I wonder where they lead, maybe to a big descent, German Wings, a crash in the mountains, or possibly Paradise where the cooking is superb and every innocent touch sets off a beautiful earthquake.

She spins and her shadow on the wall reaches out. My father's eyes open even wider.

The eyes are everything. My father breathes in and out like a woman in labour, giving birth to himself. I watch him exhale and leap into shadowland, but instead of holding her steady, he begins to turn with her so I can't tell who is who, and I can't look away.

But I do and they are gone.

"Magical thinking," the widow wrote when she dialled back the day her husband died, "See you later, Alligator," but imagine all you like, gone is gone. The music box is still. The curtain on his window moves, and I see the seagull that has been hanging around on his balcony waiting for leftovers fly off, her beak full of something, maybe the "Rose Adagio" written by a confused composer.

"He's not there," I say, turning on the overhead light when my mother wakes up and looks toward the empty bed.

"He never was," she says.

Photo: Darshan Stevens

ABOUT THE AUTHOR

Linda Rogers is a novelist, essayist, editor and songwriter, past Victoria Poet Laureate and Canadian People's Poet, and President of the League of Canadian poets and the BC Federation of Writers. She has published twenty-nine books, appeared in a number of anthologies and been awarded national and international literary prizes, including the Leacock Prize, the National Poetry Prize, the Dorothy Livesay Poetry Prize, the Gwendolyn MacEwen Prize and the Milton Acorn Award in Canada; the Cardiff Prize, the Bridport Prize and the Petra Kenney Award in Britain; the Prix Anglais in France, the Rukeyeser Award in the United States and the Voices Israel Award for Poetry.

Rogers has written songs for children with her husband, mandolinist Rick Van Krugel, who also accompanies readings, and lyrics for various songwriters. Her song for Terry Fox marked the thirtieth anniversary of his run. She wrote the screenplay for the award-winning film *Legend of the Dolphins* and the play *Warhol* for the Ontario Gallery of Art. She is currently writing a children's book, *Hello. Wiksas?* with Kwakwaka'wakw artist Chief Rande Cook, whose primary interest is also in the rights and rites of children.

Rogers writes literary criticism and profiles of many Canadian artists and is currently involved in an ekphrasis project, women poets responding to women painters, with Mexican artist Maria Luisa de Villa.

She teaches, performs and reports from Victoria, taking dictation from her crow friends.

THANKS

A few years ago, in the middle of some other tune, Michael Callaghan teased me with the challenge of writing a short story, something I had never thought of as the right music for my solo *thé dansant.*

Accustomed to sips and gulps, poems and novels, the challenge of short fiction was like asking a nude bather to wear a girdle.

Now I am addicted to *la vita breva.*

Thank you to Exile Editions, Michael, Barry, and Nina Callaghan, Gabriela Campos and Gloria Vanderbilt, for showing me that, with the right people: gloves on, veils adjusted, unmentionables mentioned, writing can be high tea.

Thank you Mother Tongue and Mona Fertig, Peter Haase, Pearl Luke, editor, and Judith Brand, copy editor, for cutting the crusts off my sandwiches. And thanks to Mark Hand for exquisite book design.

Thank you Rick for my morning coffee, the crows, the music.

"Darling Boy," "Three Strikes" and "Woolgatherer," have appeared in anthologies dedicated to Carter Vanderbilt Cooper, who flew too close to the sun. "Mouse, Not, A Sixties Scoop" appeared in the fall issue of ELQ and is nominated for a National Magazine Award, and "Three Strikes," again in the Canadian Comedy anthology, *That Damned Beaver,* Exile Editions. The Spanish translation of "One More Story" will appear in the CCLA Anthology in 2018.